GIVING MY HEART AND SOUL TO THE REALEST

Standalone

CHANIQUÉ J

ACKNOWLEDGMENTS

I always give a nice, lengthy acknowledgment in all of my books, but I'm sure y'all know just how much I appreciate yawl at this point. For me, this makes book fourteen, a lot further than what I expected. I'm going to make this short and sweet, so I don't take up too much of y'all's time.

As always, thanks to the man who makes all things possible in my life. Without prayer and faith, I don't know where I would be. Ke-Chan because you are the reason, I do what I do. I love you to the moon and back son-son. Family and Friends, you all already know I love and appreciate each and every one of you. My Publisher, Pen sisters, and other supporters, thanks for all you do to help keep me motivated. My love, of course, I had to throw you in here somewhere just because you mean that much to me not to mention you're the cover model for this book.

I hope you all enjoy this book just as you have the others. Please be sure to give feedback and leave your reviews when finished.

Sincerely,

Author Chanique J.

I've never done a dedication in any of my books and in my honest opinion Acknowledgements and Dedications are not the same so I'm going to take the time to say a few things. First, I would like to say although this book isn't about nor based on any of my relatives it's for you guys; RIP Alu "Lu" Jeter and Calvin "Beans" Carmichael. Alu you left us far before I ever started writing but the pain is still the same and when something so sudden such as Beans' death, it only refreshes the memories. Beans and you were close, and I can't help but think of how happy he is to see your face again, yet we are left here to mourn the loss of the both of you. I won't go on and on because it hurts to dwell on the death of you two, but I want you guys and everyone else to know y'all will be forever missed and yawl smiles left an impact on my heart. I Love you two more than I can explain.

SYNOPSIS

All Monee knew was DeWhite, her high school sweetheart and first love. With over ten years invested in their on again and off again relationship and two kids, Monee tried to stick it out for the sake of her family. Good just wasn't good enough for DeWhite and the family life just wasn't the thing for him. After trying time and time again to make things work Monee realized she was trying to revive a situation that was long gone. She finally walked away when she realized her first love didn't have to be her only.

When Monee met Kilo, she never expected him to be the man she would give her heart to. Agree to Disagree is pretty much what she did when she allowed him into her world. Being from two different lifestyles you would think they'd clash but surprisingly they didn't.

Kilo has always been the ladies' type of man never once settling down with just one. Keeping it real and doing what he feels is what he did best with the women he came encountered with. Kilo thought he had the game all figured out until he came across Monee.

Being fresh out of a long-term relationship that left her with nothing more than the two kids they conceived, Monee wasn't ready for what Kilo had to offer. Witnessing all the trials and tribulations her sister encountered loving Kilo's best friend, Monee begins to wonder if she bit off more than she could chew.

Everybody heard Monica's story and how she loved a boss through it all. Now it's time to take this journey along with Monee and see exactly how she fell in love, then gave her heart and soul to the realest.

It's been a long road, and I honestly don't know where to begin. This journey started three years ago with Kilo and I. When I first met him, I didn't think we would get this far. I met Kilo through my sister Monica's husband Rich. When Rich and Monica first started dating, I was introduced to Kilo. My kids' father and I were on one of our many breaks in our relationship, and Kilo only served the purpose of a good friend during that time.

Needless to say, DeWhite, my kids' dad and I got back together, and Kilo and I stopped talking. After several failed attempts to reconcile our differences and try to make things work for the sake of our kids, DeWhite and I finally split for good. At that time, I only used Kilo for someone to comfort me and help me get over my heartbreak. Just like expected, a shoulder to lean on became much more.

In the beginning, Kilo and I were only friends for at least a good two years, and I basically was in a relationship without the title. Initially, I was ok with that because I didn't want to rush into another relationship that wouldn't last. As time went by, and feelings grew stronger, I realized I wasn't ok with what we had. Knowingly, I had pretty much agreed to, without verbally agreeing, be his main chick and exclusive with him without the same treatment in return.

With any other situationship like such, it didn't last without me getting in my emotions too often or feeling as if I was being used. I would cut Kilo off for months at a time, but I always ended up back fucking with him. It's almost like Kilo wanted his cake and to eat it, too, but he didn't know how to handle the thought of settling down with just one person.

When Monica and Rich started experiencing hardships within their relationship is when Kilo and I finally started getting closer. He had finally grasped the fact that I wasn't going to tolerate the behaviors he was accustomed to. The day Monica was almost killed by Rich's side mistress Free was the start of Kilo and my relationship. From that day forward, we've been a couple and each day is different from the last. I don't know if my sister's close call with death over her husband's deranged mistress was what caused his epiphany, but whatever it was, I'm thankful he woke up before it was too late.

Chapter One

KEITH, RICH, KILO, MONEE

"How sure are you that this is the man who killed Ms. Caslin?" Detective Feeming questioned with a raised eyebrow.

"I'm almost positive. This is the man! I would've come to you sooner, but when I got the news I was incarcerated, I kind of lost it and had to finish out my time there. Meaning I wasn't able to get my early release, so I've been sitting on this information all this time."

"Yeah, because this case is almost two years old, and we've closed this case and considered it to be an unsolved homicide. We didn't have any leads, to begin with so, without any witnesses, we were basically left with nothing to go on."

"I've given you all the information I have about him, as well everything Free told me days leading up until she was killed, so I hope you're able to do something with this and get my fiancé the justice she deserves." I said, as I stood to my feet and headed out of his office.

There wasn't any need to have small talk with him because I felt like I had practically done their work while under their supervision when I was in prison. It was now time for these muthafuckas to get off their balls and make some shit happen. Leads or not, I couldn't sit back and let my bitch just be killed and nothing be done about it. That shit wasn't about to ride with me.

I'm not a snitch, nigga, but I had to do what I had to do. I needed to make sure my tracks were covered no matter what, so I wanted to go about things the legal way. We are coming up on two years since Free was killed and, although many had moved on with their lives, I hadn't. The day I got the news in my jail cell, I lost it. Free was my bitch and the mother of my children, no matter what we went through, and I still loved that woman. I couldn't believe someone would do her like that in her own home.

All types of shit ran through my mind; what if my kids were there? What if I would have been home? What if she would've moved like we planned on doing when I got out? I just felt like it could have been prevented, and I had some ounce of blame on my heart. Had I never gone to jail; I could've protected her. I've had time to sit and think of why and who would do that fucked up shit to her, and I know for a fact my story is correct. Instead of talking to people about what I thought happened or why it happened, I just kept my mouth shut until today. Doing all my time in jail meant I wasn't released on any type of papers or probation so my first stop before I saw my children was to the detective, I learned he was in charge of Free's homicide.

Free being gone left my family with our two kids. My girls were left without a mom, and I promised that I would ensure they were raised the right way and would know their momma loved them. The girls were, all Free knew, and she was a damn good mom. Her being taken away from us so soon was fucked up on so many types of levels. Looking at my girls' faces, I see nothing but Free. From her smile to her attitude when they talk.

Revenge was in my heart, but I just needed a little more time to get shit squared away, and then, shit was going hit the fan. By the time, the two-year mark rolls around, I can promise this nigga won't still be breathing, and I put that on my fiancé.

Other than trying to find a job and catching up with my nigga Pete, my life has been pretty fucked up if you ask me. The only thing that makes my life worth living is that I still have my two girls. I'm doing the best I can to be a good father but seeing them reminds me of Free so fucking much. I don't know what I would do without the help of my mom. I swear, being a single parent is harder than I could have ever imagined. It makes me feel even worse seeing how I left Free out here all alone to raise these girls by herself.

When I got out, my mom told me that Pete had been looking for me since he had got released a couple months prior. Of course, I got in contact with him, ASAP. That was my nigga for years. Shit, we even went as far as getting best friends pregnant around the same time. That tells you just how close we were. Pete and Ceeda got a little boy together named Cedric, and he's the same age as my oldest daughter.

Seeing Pete being a single father made me realize that it could be done, and although I don't wanna do it alone, I know I can. Pete has been raising Cedric on his own since he was about one. Ceeda ain't want the baby after she found out he was a boy, but she really didn't have a choice, because Pete was in jail the first year of his life.

Once he got out, he had him. The last time he went to jail, Cedric stayed with Pete's ex-girlfriend. Yeah, instead of Ceeda getting her one and only child back, she allowed another bitch to raise him. Cedric doesn't even know who his biological mother is I don't think. I've never heard him mention her or bring her up and he always referred to Pete's ex-bitch as Mom. That's a subject I try not to touch on or question about because you never know how a nigga will respond when it comes to their kids.

Pete worked with my nigga, Julian, I was locked up with and we all hung out from time to time just shooting pool, talking shit whenever we had free time. Them niggas were all for working a nine to five, but I, on the other hand, couldn't do it. I've never punched the clock for a damn soul, and I'm sure not about to start. The amount I make in a week I can make in a day on the block. Pete only has one kid to fend for and Julian doesn't have any, but I, on the other hand, have two so ain't no way that nine to five going to be enough to support us.

Whatever I do I gotta hurry up and make something shake cause my mom ain't getting no younger, and her health is starting to take a turn for the worse. doesn't have a life-threatening condition or no shit like that, but she's not able to fend for herself and my kids like she used to. She's starting to have some sort of problems with her bones, and it limits the mobility she has. The girls get a check once a month from the state for Free being dead, but I normally flip that to make the shit last us. When they turn eighteen, they both will get nice sized victims of crime check, but that's too long of a wait for some money.

As bad as I don't want to, I'm going to have to start back sticking shit. That's how I got jammed up the last time. Fuckin around with some young nigga I ain't know, and we both got caught. I told myself I would stick to hustling instead of sticking niggas up cause that shit wasn't for me but sometimes you gotta do what you gotta do.

RICH

"Am I under arrest?" I questioned the officer that was escorting me outside of my main Car Wash. Not only was this embarrassing, but it was not a good look for my business.

"No, you're not, but I need you to come down to the precinct to answer a few questions."

"Well, if I'm not under arrest, you can get your hands off of me and leave my establishment. I'll get down there when I get down there. Yawl could've called and told me to come in, instead of showing up here making a scene.

"You're not understanding what I'm saying to you. We are going to need you to come with us down to the precinct. Not come when you feel. If you choose not to, then I'm afraid I will have to place you under arrest." The officer said in a smart-alecky tone. As bad as I wanted to knock the smirk off his face, I knew that would only give them rights to kick my ass and really have something to pin on me. I couldn't think of what they would need to talk to me about. I hadn't been in the streets; all my businesses are legit, and for once in my life, I'm finally doing everything the right way.

"Aye, I'm bout to call Monica and have her get the lawyer up there. We are going to meet y'all down there." Kilo said to me as he walked towards his car. I knew Monica was going to blow a fuse when she heard I was taken downtown for questioning. The first thing I know that's going to come to her mind is that I'm hiding something from her again and that I'm sneaking hustling on the side like I once was, but I'm honestly not.

I'm pissed the police pulled this shit at my business period, but I'm thankful it was closing time, and there weren't any customers in the building, only employees. Had it been earlier in the day, there was no telling who all would have been there and witnessed the shit. Then, everybody nowadays records for Facebook, and that would've been too much negative publicity for the business. It seems like, every time a person tries to do right, something comes along and fucks it up. I couldn't do shit but sit back and wait to see what the hell they were trying to involve me with now.

I don't know how much longer they can legally hold me, but I'm over this shit. I had been sitting in the interrogation room for hours. I know it had to be the wee hours of the morning by now, and they still hadn't let me go. The clock on the wall was dead, and I didn't have my phone with me when I came down here. Two different detectives had come in and both kept questioning me about my relationship with Free. I told them stupid bitches the truth. That used to be a bitch I fucked with, but she's been dead now for a couple of years, so I ain't heard from her. I wasn't trying to be funny, but that's the truth. I knew where they were getting at with the questioning, because they asked my whereabouts the night she was killed, along with the last time I had spoken to her before I found out she was dead. Of course, I told them I didn't remember the last time we spoke; it was too far back for me to remember, and I told them I was with my wife the night she was killed.

They came at me with call logs and phone transcripts, but that shit ain't mean nothing to me. The number I had two years ago isn't the same number I have today. I'm not even with the same service provider, so I don't know what calls they are looking at. I leave that shit to the females; I don't care what a call log looks like. Just cause Free and I, at some point, had constant contact didn't mean shit. You can't prove a person killed somebody just cause they talked over the phone. I mean, how stupid does that sound?

They expected me to remember detailed events from two years ago when I can barely remember what the hell, I ate last week. I told them a little bit about our relationship, but shit, none of it was of significance, so not much about Free stuck to my memory. The night she was killed, I told them they could check with my wife. I was with her because I was comforting her because of the stunt Free pulled earlier that day. The detectives felt that was my motive behind killing her, but I stuck to my original story that I didn't kill her. As bad as I would have loved to have been the person to do it, I couldn't take credit for ending her life, but I'm not dumb enough to say nothing like that.

My guess is, after I told them I was with my wife, they contacted Monica to verify if what I was saying was true. My lawyer took forever to get here, and his damn excuse was he was out of town gambling and had to rush back to help me out. I didn't care what he was doing; that's what I paid him a retainer fee for. I kept money in his account just in case I was to ever get jammed up; he could come to my rescue.

I told them cops over and over again that I never saw Free that day, nor had I been to her house, so I didn't understand what was taking them so long to release me. I know they talk to Monica and, no matter if she and I communicated, I know how solid my wife is. Plus, she has a legal background so she's far from dumb.

"Mr. Pickens, you're free to go home for now." The detective came into the room and released me.

"Shit, you saying for now, but we both know y'all ain't got nothing on me," I said and gave his bitch ass the same smirk he gave me.

I don't know what made these muthafuckas come looking for me two years after some shit happened, but I'm not about to worry about it. I know that I did and what I didn't do, so they can pin that bitch's murder on the next nigga. I'm not a sloppy nigga, and if there was any evidence against me, then they would have come to me sooner. Somebody was behind this, and if I got to go on a manhunt until whoever it is, shows face, then that's exactly what I'm going to do.

KILO

Two years later and they want to randomly come after my nigga like he is the killer or some shit. I couldn't believe how they came in the car wash acting like they owned shit demanding Rich come down for questioning right then and there. That was the first time I ever saw some shit like that. Normally, if you're not under arrest, you're allowed to come down on your own time at your own will, but they were threatening to arrest him right then and there if he didn't comply.

I immediately called up our lawyer Mike Shalomski and told him Rich needed him down at the precinct. My next call was to Monica. I really didn't want to be the one to tell her because I hated to be the bearer of bad news, but sis needed to know. Of course, like expected, she immediately flipped out thinking the worst. She thought that Rich had done some shit and got jammed up, but I told her I honestly didn't know why they came because bro hadn't been into any types of situations that would cause him to be in any type of legal trouble.

Monica ended up dropping the baby off at Monee's and meeting me downtown. We ended up waiting for almost three hours then the detectives came and got Monica saying she needed to be questioned as well. I thought since they were married, that was against the spousal privilege for them to testify against each other. I immediately called Shalomski up and told him he needed to hurry his ass because they were doing all types of illegal shit just to build a case against Rich.

Although I still didn't know what they were questioning him about, I knew something wasn't right. Rich never did anything that would put Monica in the middle, so for them to question her, I was confused as hell. They hadn't even looked my way, and Rich and I are hand in hand when it comes to everything. Of all people, I expected for them to question me, but they didn't.

Shortly after Shalomski got there and said what he had to say, they released Rich and Monica. We waited until we were out of the precinct before we said a word to each other. Anything you say, they can flip and try to build a case against you, and we didn't need to help them out any. Shalomski suggested we meet up at his office, which was also located downtown. When Rich said they had brought him in about Free's murder, that shit blew my mind. It ain't make no sense to me why they would wait damn near two years to come questioning him and trying to pin some shit on him.

I knew that Rich didn't have a thing to do with that murder, but he needed to prove that to them. Which I didn't understand why, but that's just how the judicial system works. They ended up questioning Monica to verify that Rich's story was valid about him being with Monica when the murder took place. Monica went along with saying Rich was with her, and she didn't even know what was going on. That's one thing I have to give Monica; she's solid in every situation when it comes to Rich, even at times when she shouldn't have been. Rich did right by getting his shit together for the sake of his and Monica's relationship. She's the definition of a true rider. She got my bro's back for real.

"Where the hell have you been, and why are you just now getting here? It's damn near three o'clock in the morning. I have been calling your phone for hours. All I know is Monica dropped Micah off saying something about Rich. She never said you were jammed up too, so why haven't you at least texted me? That's what I be talking about, Kilo... our level of communication sucks. You gotta do better." Monee was steady running her damn mouth not even knowing why she was bitching.

"Man, Monee ain't nobody trying to hear that. You running your mouth and getting all worked up for nothing. You know damn well anything dealing with Rich, nine times out of ten, involves me as well. Who the hell you think called Monica? I ain't have time to call you cause I ain't know what the fuck was going on."

"Whatever, Kilo. Like I said, you gotta do better. I ain't know what the hell was going on with you or if shit was ok or not." Monee replied with a slight attitude.

"Well, you knew shit wasn't too bad because your sister would have called and let your nosey ass know. Babe, trust me, if I was in any type of situation where I wasn't ok, I would make sure you knew. Calm down. Alright?"

"I'm calm, Kilo. I'm just being concerned about my man. Ain't I supposed to be concerned about you?" Monee asked.

"You good, babe. Just don't be trippin like that soon as I walk in the damn door." I said laughing. Monee was a firecracker, and she knew it.

"I be trying not to, but you can't have me all worried and not knowing what's going on when it comes to you." She was trying to justify her fly ass mouth but wasn't no justification for it.

"Listen, the police came and got Rich and started questioning him about Free's murder. They're trying to pin it on him, but he's innocent. We ended up being down there for that entire time; they even questioned Monica. I don't know what the hell is going on or what was said to the detectives for them to come looking after all this time, but they're trying to build a case. The only beneficial part is that Rich is innocent so they going to fuck around and waste their time fucking with us.

"What? Are you serious? Why do you think they waited so long if they didn't have any information? Do you think they know who really did it? Do you think somebody told them that Rich did it?" Monee was now looking like a deer in headlights asking question after question.

"Honestly, I don't know who said what. All I know is Rich is innocent, and that's it, that's all. I'm done talking about this tonight. I've had enough of this dead bitch for the day."

MONEE

"Babe, what if I told you something that I've been keeping to myself for the past two years? How would you feel?" I questioned Kilo.

"Shit, it honestly depends on exactly what you're about to tell me. You better pick your words wisely, Nee, cause I don't mind goin upside your muthafuckin head." Kilo said in a serious yet joking manner. I didn't know how to take him, but I knew I needed to get this shit off my chest and quick.

"Ok, babe, can you promise me that, no matter what I'm about to tell you, you will keep this between the two of us no matter what?"

"Stop beating around the damn bush and just say it. What, you scared I'm gonna call up Rich, soon as you walk out the room like you and Monica do whenever we talk?" Kilo started laughing, but I was busted. I didn't know that he actually knew that me and Monica told each other everything, even the shit we weren't supposed to when it came to Kilo and Rich.

"I'm not beating around the bush so shut up. And I don't call and tell my sister everything. There are some things I keep just between me and you like I need this secret to be."

"Man, Nee, come on and say the shit before you piss me off. You dragging this one too long. Look, I'm not about to tell no damn body, ok? Happy now? I said it. Your secret is safe with me." Kilo's ass never knew how to stay serious, but I believed him when he told me my secret was safe.

"Ok, here goes nothing. I killed Free." I blurted out. Then, I let out a sigh of relief because it felt like a weight had just been lifted off my shoulders.

"Wait, you did what? Stop fucking playing with me, Monee." Kilo stood up and his eyes were big as saucers. It's almost like he didn't believe what I was trying to tell him.

"I did, I killed her. I had to. She was going after my sister, and I felt like the only way she was going to stop was if she was dead. I knew Monica wouldn't do it, and I was fed up at that point. She had been pushing my sister for far too long, and I couldn't sit back and watch her continue to hurt Monica like that. Monica didn't deserve the shit Free was putting her through."

"Monee, say you swear to God, you did that shit?" Kilo asked as he rubbed his hand across his forehead and began to pace the floor.

"Yea... Yeah. I did it. I didn't know what else to do."

"I can't even blame you because, if somebody did some of the things she did to Rich, I would send them to their maker, too, but I ain't think you had that shit in you. Monee, listen, this is something we are going to have to keep between us. That means don't tell a soul, not even Monica. I know you said you've kept the secret this long, but this is something you need to continue to keep."

"Ok, I will." I said in a nonchalant tone.

I wanted to tell Monica the moment I did it, but I had been scared she would run back and tell Rich. I'm not saying he would tell anyone, but I didn't want anyone to know. This was something that could change the rest of my life. I could be sent to prison and taken away from my kids for the rest of my life, and I just can't do that. After Monica called and told me that they were taken down for questioning, I knew I had to come clean. I wouldn't allow anyone else to take the fall for what I did, even though I didn't want to go down either. I really didn't know what to do at this point, and that was the reason I was telling Kilo instead of telling my sister. I knew Kilo would know how to handle this.

"Man, all alone, we have been thinking that nigga Keith had some-body kill her for fucking around with Rich and was just trying to cover his tracks, but it's all starting to make sense now." Kilo let out a chuckle and walked over towards me.

"Now, just cause you got away with that shit don't mean you are the bitch from Tomb raider or no shit like that. Don't get any other ideas before running them by me first. Oh, and don't even think about trying no crazy shit with me cause you met your match this time buddy." Kilo said before kissing my forehead and laughing as he walked away.

"Shut up, babe, I would never do nothing to hurt you like that." I yelled in his direction.

"That shit done fucked my head up. I need a damn drink now fucking with you." Kilo said, and I knew that meant he was in the kitchen pouring him a cup of D'usse.

I felt like a weight was lifted off my shoulders, and I could breathe but, then again, I'm worried cause it's going to be on Kilo's brain. I don't want him to start thinking I'm some mass murderer or nothing like that, cause I'm not a killer, but don't push me. I did what any sister would have done, and I would do it again if I had to when it comes to Monica. Monica don't bother anybody, and that's how she's always been. It's eating at me to have to keep this from my sister because I am in fact my sister's keeper, but Monica's so soft when it comes to Rich. I know for a fact she will fuck around and run her mouth to him. Kilo is the only person I can trust to keep this, and hopefully, I made the right decision by telling him.

Chapter Two

KILO, MONICA, MONEE, DEWHITE

I couldn't believe the shit Monee hit me with the other night. Ever since then, I been low-key looking at my bae a little differently. I never pictured her to be the killer type, but then again, you never know what a person is capable of doing when pushed to the point where they have no other choice. She was protecting what she loved, and I don't blame her for doing it. I just wish she would have come to me instead of doing it by herself. There was no telling if she handled it the best way possible. I mean, it's been two years, and they still really don't know who did it or have any solid evidence, so she did something right, but all it takes is for her to have one minor slip-up and it's a wrap.

Before I see my woman take the fall on a murder wrap, I'll take the charge. Monee got too much to live for, and she's not built for jail. She's a good woman with two kids she's raising. I can't see her throw her life away like that. I've never been the type of nigga to give much of shit to a woman but, for Monee, I'll throw my freedom away just because I care that much for her, and I honestly believe in my heart she would do it for me. Although I would never ask her to do such a thing, it's the principle.

Rich and I had been talking to Shalomski trying to figure out who was out to get him, but that information hadn't been given. We knew it had to be a hating ass nigga in the cut somewhere out for bad, because the shit was so random, and it wasn't making much sense. Rich kept saying he wasn't worried about it because he knew he was innocent, but I was. Not only did I know how the system worked, but I knew that my woman was the one responsible for it. The fear of the truth coming out somehow is what had me trying to get to the bottom of it. I didn't tell Rich what Monee told me, because the fewer people who know, the less I have to worry. Not that I didn't trust Rich, but some things you just have to keep to yourself and between you and your mate; this was one of those things.

It's obvious, at this point, that Monee and I aren't your average couple, so the normal secrets couples have we didn't have... more like rap sheets, and murders. The shit sounds funny but it's true. Monee knew about all the dirt I did in my past and the shit I did that I wasn't proud of, but they made me the man I am today. That's why I fucked with her so hard because she didn't pass judgment from the beginning and still stuck around to hold a fucked-up individual like me down.

It took us a nice little minute to get to the point where we are now because I just couldn't see myself settling down but, after a few years of seeing her loyalty, I knew I couldn't lose her. For a woman to remain loyal to a nigga that's not ever technically hers, it showed just how loyal she could be. Not many women can even remain faithful to the nigga they with, let alone just some nigga they fucking, but Monee proved me she could.

Monee is the type of woman you want and need on your team, so if you run across a rare breed like her, you gotta lock her down before it's too late.

"How long, you about to be up here? I gotta make a run to one of the other buildings, and then, I gotta take Monica and baby girl something to eat." Rich walked into my office taking me out of my thoughts.

"I'll be here for a little minute. I still got a lot more shit to get done. I'm sure I'll still be here when you get back unless something comes up. If it does, though, I'll call you and let you know."

"Ok, bet. Aye, some chick just walked in, too. I think she may need some help, but I gotta run." Rich said and was out just like that. That nigga always wanna run for cover when customers come. I swear, he is the most antisocial businessman I fucking know.

I got up from behind my desk and headed to the front because we only had a few workers here today, and they were all outside handling other duties.

"How, you doing today? Can I help you with anything?" I greeted the woman who had just walked in and was standing at the counter looking as if she was on the way to the club instead of the car wash.

"Yes, you can, actually. I'm looking to have my car fully detailed. Do yawl have any specials going on right now?" She asked while leaning down on the counter, so her cleavage could spill out some from the low-cut shirt she had on. I had to remind myself I was a taken man now and off the market, cause shawty was definitely my type. The easy and frisky ones who I know won't take much to hit and quit.

"We can get that done for you. We are actually running a few specials right now. Are you looking to have the outside as well inside detailed?" I questioned hoping to get a better understanding of exactly what she needed to be done.

"Ummm. I'm thinking I want both done." She said and licked her lips. I felt my man's waking up because I pictured her wrapping those lips around my head. I had to adjust myself in my pants discreetly, because she was getting my attention, and that wasn't a good thing. I'm glad I was standing on the opposite side of the counter or my cover would have been for sure blown.

"I may need something else, too, if yawl offer that type of service. What's your name, by the way? You never told me that." *Yeah, Shawty definitely in go mode,* I thought to myself.

"My fault; I'm Kilo. What other services would you be needing to be done?" I asked with a raised eyebrow. She was really trying me.

"My other services wouldn't include any cleaning; it would only involve me and you." Oh yeah, she was bold as fuck coming in somebody's place of business and trying to throw the pussy that quick.

"Ha, well actually..."

"So, this why the fuck you can't answer the phone, cause you in here cheesing and shit in the next hoe face?" I was cut off by Monee storming in the front doors with a mean ass grill on her face. She ain't give two fucks if it was a customer or not the way she came in here talking shit.

"Nee, calm down." I tried to defuse her before she got too close to the customer.

"Nah, don't tell her to calm down. She came in this bitch talking strong cause you helping a customer that's shitting on her whole existence."

"See that's..." Monee cut my ass off once again. I know I didn't have to stand up for her, but I wasn't gonna let this thot ass bitch disrespect her.

"Nah, bae, I got this. What you not going do is disrespect me in my man's business in my face or behind my back. I say that shit cause you look like the thirsty type of bitch that would come in this bitch trying to throw your pussy around for a free car wash or some shit. What you can do is grab your keys to that beat-up ass Honda outside I'm sure is yours and beat your fucking feet." Monee said as she walked around the counter and stood on the side of me.

"Your man, huh? It's funny; he never mentioned he had a woman. Oh, and as far as I'm concerned, this ain't your business, so I ain't gotta go nowhere. He ain't said shit; that's all you running your mouth."

"Look, bitch, I'm trying my hardest to keep it chill with your ass cause, like I said, this is his business but you pushing it. See this." Monee grabbed my dick by my pants with her right hand. "All this is me whether he said something or not. It's not his job to explain his relationship status to every customer; it's to sell your ass the service that's offered which ain't him.

"Listen, enough of all this. Unfortunately, we can't be of any service to you. So, I would appreciate it if you grabbed your keys and took your business elsewhere." I said and shooed her away like the fuckin peasant she was being. I had enough of her mouth and the slick talk. I knew it was only a matter of seconds before Monee took off on her, and I ain't want that to take place in the lobby. The last thing I needed was for my woman to be in here fighting. Shit, we would fuck around and jump this bitch whether Monee was beating her ass or not. That's all bad for business, so the best thing to do was to ask her to leave the premises. I guess she was offended cause she turned her nose up and snatched her keys off the counter before being on her merry little way.

Monee always talked shit about showing up and showing out, but I had never seen her act this way before. At first, I was low-key pissed she did it, but after a few minutes, that shit made my dick hard, especially when she cupped my shit claiming what's hers without ever thinking twice. Monee just didn't know that little stunt had me ready to bend her over the counter right here right now in broad daylight. Cameras and all; if it wasn't for other employees being on duty, I would've done it.

"Nigga don't make me fuck your black ass up in here. Make that the last time I call your damn phone and you don't answer or text back cause you with a thot ass customer. If I wouldn't have walked in, that thirsty hoe would've been on this counter with her pussy on display for a car wash." Monee said as she pointed her finger in my face. I just bit the corner of my lip and gave her a seductive smile.

"Ain't shit cute or funny." Monee said and smiled before giving me a kiss on my lips. I was callin to tell your ass I was dropping off my car and taking your truck cause I need an oil change." Her ass thought she was slick. Ain't nobody tell her to just come and put claims on my truck like it was hers.

"Damn, you wasn't going to ask me for my truck? You were just going to come take my shit?" I joked with her. I really didn't care cause I wasn't about to go anywhere, but I had to play the role of being tough.

"Babe, where are your keys? I gotta go get the kids. Plus, your Yukon looks way better than my little Trailblazer. I like riding in your truck more than I like mine." Monee pouted.

"So, what you saying is you want a new car basically?" I gave her ass the side-eye.

"I'm not saying that, but if you wanna get me a new one, I would be forever grateful." Monee gave me a schoolgirl smile trying to wheel me in.

"Man, get your spoiled ass out of her. Call me after you get the kids. I'mma have one of the guys go drop your car off at the dealership to get the oil change; they don't have much work to do out there anyway."

"That's coo. I'll call you in a minute bae." Monee said before giving me a kiss goodbye and heading right back out those same doors she had just come in minutes prior.

MONICA

It's a true fact that when things seem to be going too good something is brewing. Rich and I hadn't had any problems since Free died and somehow, someway this bitch even was interrupting my life in death. She's been dead far too long for me to even have thought something revolving around her would come up and stir up some shit.

I haven't been able to function right since the day Kilo called telling us that the police had come to pick Rich up from their business. It's like I fear that, at any given moment, they are going to come in and take my husband from me. In my heart, I feel like Rich didn't do it, but I don't know for sure. I'm scared to ask him because I'm scared of what his answer might be.

The detectives ended up questioning me as well and they did so before I even had a chance to speak with Rich. They knew all about the arson shit she had pulled earlier in the day when she tried to kill me, but their storyline as far as her death was still very unclear. Working in a law firm for all those years, I knew a little something about how the court system worked. No, I didn't work with criminal cases, but I knew the process. If their case was strong enough, they would have already taken Rich but that doesn't mean they won't do whatever it takes to build a strong enough case and come back like they are trying to do now.

The night Free got killed, I was at the hotel, and Rich did call me saying it was over and he wanted his family back. I didn't know what that meant exactly when the words came out of his mouth, but when he came to comfort me, and we watched the news together, I had a clear understanding. Knowing the shit Rich would say and threaten to do, I thought for a long while that he did it, but my heart wouldn't allow me to believe it. Even if he did do it, I would never tell, on my husband. Not only would that be betrayal to him, but my family as well.

Rich and I have a daughter to worry about now, and I would never take her father away from her. Especially not to serve justice for a bitch who created so much chaos in my life.

The detective by the name of Feeming kept pressuring me to say that Rich wasn't with me the entire night of the killing, but I stuck to my word. Whether it was a lie or not I would keep that secret from them until the death of me. As far as I was concerned, Rich was with me from the time of the fire incident until the following morning when we checked out of the hotel. The detectives didn't know we weren't living together during that time, nor did they know that my marriage was practically over until I got wind that Free was dead. Had they known all of those facts; they would've felt the motive behind Free's death was indeed strong enough to pin everything on Rich.

If I could, I would bring that bitch back from the dead and kill her stankin ass again for all the fucking bullshit she continues to put my family through. If I knew who her family was, I would make sure to make their life a living hell just because that's what someone is trying to do with mine. Instead of worrying about this nonsense, I should be worrying about the planning of my daughter's first birthday.

Micha will be one next month, and I can't even focus like I want to. Monee and Egypt told me not to worry about the planning part because they were going to plan; I just needed to give them the money. Thank goodness for a great support system because Lord knows I need their help. Micha has been trying to walk lately, and she's into every-thing. She's taking one or two steps then she gives up. The only way she will walk far is if she is holding onto something. Rich gets mad every time she falls down talking about, I need to catch her, but I told him, if she doesn't fall, she doesn't learn. He's so overprotective of that little girl it annoys my soul.

"Bae what, you in there cooking? Me and baby girl are starving." Rich complained.

"I was making some Chicken Alfredo, but I'm done now. I'll be in there in a second; I'm making yawl's plates now."

"Good, hurry up. Our stomachs touching our backs. We are starting to look like the kids on those hungry commercials." Rich said and started laughing.

"Man, get the hell outta here. I ain't even been in here that long." I yelled back into the living room where they were sitting watching cartoons.

"Tell mommy, tummy hurts." Rich advised Micha.

"Mommy...tummy," Micha said trying to repeat what her dad instructed her to.

"Yawl two so darn dramatic. Here I come." I said as I grabbed the tray with both of their plates on it. Micha would be sitting in her highchair, but I always served them at the same time. I don't believe in my man-eating before my child or my child eating before my husband. In our household, we are all equal.

"Damn, bae, not only does this shit smell amazing, but this shit looks and tastes just as good." Rich yelled from the living room in my direction. I was heading back into the kitchen to get my food, so I could join my family in eating dinner. Although we have a fully furnished dining room, we normally eat in the living room in front of the TV. I think it's more comfortable and Rich just likes watching TV while he eats. He always complains that sitting in the dining room is only for holidays. I don't know where he got that logic because it made no sense to me.

"I'm glad you like it. I tried some new seasonings. I wasn't sure how it was going to turn out." I said while sitting down and putting a forkful of Alfredo into my mouth. "Love, there's something we need to talk about." I broke the silence as we were eating.

"What's up, babe?" Rich said with his eyes still fixed on the TV.

"I'm pregnant." I said, nonchalantly.

"Fa real?" Rich said in an excited tone and faced me with one of the biggest smiles on his face. It's obvious he felt completely opposite of what I did.

"I'm dead ass serious." I said and continued to eat my food.

"Why, you don't seem happy about this, babe?"

"Cause, honestly, I'm not. I don't know if we are ready for another baby so soon, Rich."

"What, you mean you don't think we are ready? We are married, financially stable, and doing damn good if you ask me. What else do we really need to work on? I'm lost. Please explain this to me so I can understand where you're coming from." Rich said with a confused look on his face. I could tell I low-key pissed him off and hurt his feelings at the same time.

"It's not about the financial part, nor our marriage, babe. It's just Micha is just about to turn one and another baby means starting all over. What if we can't give both kids the same amount of attention. Micha is still a baby technically. Then, we have all this shit going on with the detectives. What if they come back with some other shit and try to take you to jail?"

"So, that's what your resistance is all about? Don't blame it on Micha being a baby still. The truth is, you're scared I'm going get jammed up, and you're going to be out here raising them on your own. Just say the shit."

"I mean I. I'm." I stuttered but Rich cut me off before I could say much more.

"Nah, don't try to switch it up now. Monica, I know you, and I know when you're bullshitting. I'm your husband, and you trust me when I tell you that I got this, right?" Rich questioned me.

"I do trust you, but...." Micha was sitting there eating her food looking back and forth between the two of us as if she really understood what we were talking about.

"There shouldn't be no buts. Either you trust me, or you don't. When I told you I was innocent, I was being one hundred percent honest with you. Do you really think I would lie to you about something so serious and put my family in harm's way? As bad as I wish I was the person who did it, I can't take that credit." Rich fumed. He was no longer as calm as he was when we initially started this conversation.

"I'm sorry, babe. I'm not saying I don't trust or believe you. I only know that you called me and said it was done, and we started working on repairing our marriage. I know she's dead, but I don't know who killed her, and I didn't think anyone else would want her dead as much as we did when all of that took place." Rich gave me a look like he was ready to tear my head off.

"Listen, we are done with this conversation cause, you talking too crazy in front of Micha."

"She doesn't even know what we are talking about, Rich."

"You don't know what she understands. You see her following us like a damn ping pong game. I told you I didn't do it, and that's that. Now, if that's the reason for you not wanting our child, you are going to have to come up with some other excuse, cause that shit ain't going to cut it for me." Rich stood to his feet and headed to the kitchen with his and Micha's empty plate in hand.

"You're putting words in my mouth, babe."

"Nah, you the one said you ain't want it."

"You're saying that like I'm going get rid of it or something."

"You ain't stupid. Trust me, I know you ain't going to do no stupid shit like that."

"Alright, Rich, I'm not trying to argue with you. I'm scheduling our first appointment tomorrow."

"Yeah, do that, and let me know what day it is so Kilo can cover the shops."

MONEE

"Did you really expect me to be single forever? I mean, I allowed you to move on and do you or whatever you're over there doing without ever saying a word. Why are you trying to hold me back from moving on with my life?"

"What, you mean? We broke up and agreed to take a break until I had my mind right, and now, you wanna switch it up. When we separated, we agreed we would work on us and make things work for the kids. This shit was only supposed to be temporary, and now you are telling me you're just done for good?"

"No, that's where you're wrong. I never agreed to shit. That was you had in your head. What I did say was we would work on things for the kids, meaning make things work in their best interest. Us being together wasn't healthy for them. See, the way we were isn't how kids are supposed to grow up. The negativity isn't the type of atmosphere I wanted my kids around, and you said you understood that.

Obviously, you misunderstood what I was saying. When we broke up, I planned on that being for good. You've had time to get your mind right since before we had kids. How much fucking time did you think I was going to give you? I gave you ample opportunity to do right by me and your kids and you ruined it. Now, my only concern is that you continue to be the father you have been to them."

"Fuck outta here, Monee. You really think this co-parenting thing is going to last?" DeWhite questioned me.

"Ahhh, yeah. Why wouldn't it work? Shit, you've actually been a better father now that we aren't together than you were when we lived together."

"So what, you trying to say? I wasn't a good dad before this little breakup?"

"No, what I'm saying is your relationship with the kids has improved tremendously. Now the time you spend with them is focused on them and not us as a whole. Before you moved out when was the last time you actually spent quality time with the kids? My point, I can't remember, and I'm sure you don't either. The kids are happier, and so am I at this point. It is what it is, DeWhite, and this is what it's going to be. There is no more you and me."

"Fuck it, Monee. I'm not about to beg you nor kiss your ass. I've done more than enough of that over the years. But what you're not about to do is play house with my fucking kids and your new nigga. You're up and moving and can't even tell me where to. How am I supposed to know my kids are ok when they with whoever the fuck you dealing with. Don't let whoever he is get to your fucking head?"

"Me moving has nothing to do with the kids. I'm moving because this house was the house we shared, and I'm not about to continue to stay here with our memories when I've moved on with my life. You should trust me enough to know I'm not about to allow any man to be around my kids that I can't trust. The kids know him and have been around him for some time now. It's not like I just rushed into this, and I've actually talked to the kids about this decision before just up and making it. What you aren't about to do is tell me how to raise my kids when I'm their primary caregiver." I said before hanging up in his fucking face.

I had had enough of DeWhite's ass for the day. I already took enough of my time away from packing to have that stupid ass conversation with him. I wasn't about to waste another second explaining to him why I didn't want to be with him and why we were moving.

I had been packing and throwing shit away for over a month, and it still seemed like I had so much to do. I threw away more than half of the shit we had, because I wanted to start fresh, and I still couldn't see the finish line. Other than the kids' stuff, clothes, photos, and stuff like that, practically everything was in the trash pile or gone already. There was no way I would be hauling old furniture that I had when DeWhite lived here to a place I would be living with Kilo in. Not only was Kilo not having it, I didn't want to carry the memories with me. It was one thing to have those things still in this house, but a whole other to take them with me.

It was already a task to get Kilo to let go of his place. For some reason, he felt like he still needed to have his bachelor's pad. We had been going at it about that for months until he finally gave in. I told him there was no way in hell we would be moving into a house that we are both paying the mortgage on and he still has a whole lease elsewhere. Like, if we are trying to make things work and move forward from this point on, what is the purpose of him having his own place? It's not like I'm keeping mine, so it's not fair for him to keep his.

The only excuse Kilo could give me was that he refused to be homeless if I ever kicked him out. I explained to him that, even if we were to argue, legally I couldn't kick him out if his name was on the mortgage as well. Finally, he gave in, because I told him we wouldn't be moving anywhere together if we both weren't letting go of our places. What I was trying to get through Kilo's head was, when you get in a relationship, you turn all your "I's" into "we's". There are no longer decisions you make based off your choices alone; you need to consider the other person at all times.

I don't think I could mentally handle it if Kilo kept his place. I would be insecure as fuck. Like, what is the purpose? Are you sneaking other bitches over there or going there when you don't wanna come home? All types of shit would be running through my head. Shit, I already be ready to pull my damn hair out and cut a damn fool when he doesn't come in at night here, and he technically didn't even live here. He only had a key and clothes here, but we technically never considered him to live here because this was once DeWhite and my home.

Just as I was about to grab the last trash bag of clothing from the basement, I heard my phone chime. I knew it was a text message because of the alert tone. I'm hoping it is Kilo saying he's on the way to help. He's at the other house now unloading the U-Haul with the help of Rich and their other friend Doe. Unfortunately, when I picked up the phone, I read DeWhite's name instead of Kilo's. I can only imagine what the hell he has to say after me hanging up on him. Sometimes, DeWhite can be such a bitch, and I wonder how we lasted as long as we did.

DeWhite: *When it comes to these kids, they are mine, too, and if we can't come to some sort of understanding, I don't mind taking you to court for them. Shit, the judge needs to know how you got some thug all around my kids anyway.*

Me: *What you not about to do is threaten me when it comes to MY fucking kids. You don't know who I have around them so speak on what you know and not what you heard. You're the one going to look real stupid when you got to pay child support. Do what you feel stupid ass. Either way, my decision remains the same. Now have a blessed day.*

DeWhite: *I don't know what this nigga did to you that got you acting like a straight bitch, but you need to fix the shit and quick.*

Me: *Tootles DeWhite.*

If it wasn't for that stupid ass nigga having my kids right now, I would put his punk ass on the block list and for good. He's irritating my entire soul acting the way he is. I've tried to be nice but, for some reason, he just wasn't getting the point. Like, I don't want to be with you now, or later, so get it through your head. It's not like I hate him because I will always love him. I just refuse to put myself back in that situation ever again. DeWhite wasn't terrible but the family life wasn't for him, and the sad part is, it was the family he helped me to create.

If it wasn't for Ceeda telling me about Monee and Kilo being together, I would have never known who Monee was dating because the kids weren't telling me, and Monee sure as hell wasn't. She said she didn't feel as if it was any of my business who she was dating as long as he treated our kids with respect. I understood where she was coming from to a certain extent. She never knew who I was fucking with, but that's only because she didn't ask. I'm sure she asked other people, but she never asked me.

It's totally different for a man, in my opinion, because if I'm trying to be an active father. I should know everything that's going on where my kids lay their head. As far as I'm concerned, the nigga lives with them. My bitches have never lived with me, so my kids aren't around them as much.

There's no way in hell I believe that Monee has moved on completely with her life. I think she's just using Kilo as a pastime or to make me jealous. I don't give a fuck who says what or how hard she tried to act because I knew the real Monee. We were together for over ten years and have two kids together. I know her better than any man will ever know her. That's why I'm so shocked she's acting the way she is. Acting all brand-new all of a sudden doesn't convince me, so she can take that tough acting shit elsewhere. This entire time we have been separated, she's been mad coo, and we haven't argued once. I mean, she's cussed me out a few times because I tried to fuck her but nothing too serious, until now.

Anyways, back to Ceeda telling me about Monee. Ceeda and I had been fucking around since a little after Free died. We ain't nothing serious or a couple, but that's the only chick I been fucking with on a constant basis. She's mad coo, and I like how laid-back she is. She's not on my shit and down my back like a lot of females are nowadays. She allows me to have my space and she respects the fact I'm not trying to be with anyone right now exclusively. Granted, she's the only bitch I'm fuckin, I still talk to other bitches and get my dick sucked from time to time.

My plan was to originally get my family back by the time my lease was up at the two-bedroom apartment I got, but that shit doesn't look like it is happening. This was the first time in my life that I had lived alone and, honestly, I'm over the shit. I like coming home to a cooked meal and a clean house. Having to take care of all that shit on my own is a hassle, especially when I have the kids. Most of the time, when I have them, we eat fast food and live like a bunch of savages. My kids are still young being only five and seven, so there's always toys every damn where.

My kids love the fact that they have "two homes" as they call it, but the shit is driving me crazy. I don't like the idea of them living with any man other than myself. I don't want them getting too comfortable and calling another man dad or pops. That shit pisses me off just thinking about it. My daughter Danee already be talking about how nice her mom's boyfriend is and how much she likes him. Next thing you know, she'll be saying that's her stepdad. My son Jr really doesn't speak on much when it comes to what goes on at their mom's house, and I'm sure that's because she's programmed him well enough. Either way, it goes, I'm not happy with the situation going on in her household.

I need to come up with a plan to put all this shit to an end and quick. I don't know how I'm going to do it because Monee is really acting fly, all of a sudden. Until I can figure it out, I'm going to have to try my hardest to keep my feelings in a can, because I can't afford for her to keep my kids from me over her personal feelings.

"Babe, this is my bro Keith and his daughters, Salina and Kenitha. Salina is five, like Danee, and is about to be eight." Ceeda introduced me to her brother and his kids. We were at Chuck e Cheese with the kids and my guess is she called him up here, so the kids would have some other kids to play with. I appreciated the gesture, but she should've warned me.

"What's up; I'm DeWhite. My daughter Danee and son Jr are somewhere around here running around. I'm sure you'll see them here shortly." I said to the dude Keith as I shook his hand.

"I'll go find them. I gotta get my nieces some tokens anyways. Yawl two can sit here and chop it up and get to know each other a little better." Ceeda said in a happy tone. I don't know why the hell she was so excited about me meeting her people, cause we weren't anything serious. Shit, and if you ask me, we weren't going to be either.

"I don't know why Ceeda thinks we kids or some shit. She's always trying to tell somebody what to do like we ain't grown ass men." Keith joked.

"That's Ceeda for you. Always gotta be the center of something." I replied.

"Man, tell me about it. She's been like this since I can remember. But I appreciate y'all inviting us out. My girls don't really have too many kids to play with other than each other. It's been hard for me just getting out of jail and trying to entertain them. I'm a man; I know nothing about Barbie's and easy bake ovens, but I'm trying." Keith said while shaking his head.

"I can feel where you're coming from, but I'm thankful to have a Jr. My daughter is real to herself for the most part. She doesn't really want me or her brother to interfere with her when she's playing. I guess that's because she's used to being the only girl. My son is a game head, so we got that in common, thank God." I briefly explained my relationship with my kids to carry on with our conversion.

Keith and I ended up chopping it up for a nice amount of time while Ceeda entertained the kids. Ceeda had some good qualities in her, but I just couldn't see myself making her my woman. Her rap sheet and ways just weren't what I think qualified as wifey material. There's a difference between wifey and a girlfriend; she fit one but not the other. At this time in my life, I'm not trying to have a girlfriend. I need a wifey. I have kids. and the only woman I see fitting that position is Monee.

When it was time to leave, the girls were pretty disappointed. They weren't ready to separate. I knew Danee wouldn't be because she's always around her brother, but she understood it was time to go home. I needed to get them home and to bed. We stayed until it was damn near closing time. Keith, Ceeda, and I all agreed to allow the kids to meet up again soon for another play date since they played so well together. My son really didn't care, because they were all girls, which I figured he wouldn't care if we left or not because he's just laid back like that when it comes to certain stuff.

Chapter Three

KILO, MONEE, MONICA, KILO

The time had finally come, and I was really turning in my keys, to my bachelor's pad and moving all my shit into a house Monee and I would share. I had never officially lived with a woman. I mean, I've stayed with Monee but never moved in completely. The first reason being I refused to move into a house that both our names weren't on the lease. Secondly, I always told myself when I moved again, I would be purchasing the next place instead of renting. The last and most important reason is that, at some point, Monee and her baby's dad used to share that house. What type of nigga would I look like moving into a house that was once his? No matter how much redecorating we did, it still was once his and hers.

My original plan was to keep my place no matter what because I felt like Monee would at some point try some funny shit, and I would have to leave and go back home. Before I allow a chick to put me out and leave me looking stupid, I could always go back to my own home. Monee had been stressing for the past year that I let it go and, if the house we were purchasing had both of our names on the deed, then she wouldn't legally be able to put me out. She felt that, if I kept another place outside of ours, I wouldn't come home on certain nights.

She said it would be a bachelor's pad for whenever we argued or fought, and I would have hoes up and through there. I can't lie, the thought ran through my mind, but I wouldn't really do it. I had enough time to have hoes up and through my place, and I'm not on the shit right now. I don't even have the time of day to entertain a bunch of hoes like I used to, now that I'm with Monee.

Finally, I gave in and decided that in order to build an empire with the woman I plan to be with, I gotta let certain shit go. I had already let go of the best thing... the one thing I thought I would never get tired of and that's random pussy. If I could remain faithful, then I'm sure it wouldn't be that hard to let go of a place I barely slept at.

I allowed Monee to do all the furniture shopping and to decorate. Of course, she and Monica had a field day out spending my money freely. I didn't care because that means the only thing I had to do was decorate my man cave, the only area of the house I wouldn't dare allow her to put her personal touch on. I needed to have a space in the house that I could get away from any and everything if shit got too hectic. Monee, I'm sure, would use our room as her little getaway area, which was fine with me.

The kids had separate rooms and a playroom so there was no excuse for them to be in my personal space. D-Man as I call Monee's son has his own thirty-two-inch TV in their playroom with his game systems, and Danee has her own thirty-two-inch TV to watch whatever she wants. That way, they have no reason to fuss or fight over what's going on in the playroom. Monee said they couldn't have TVs in their room, or it would be a problem when it was time for bed. As bad as I wanted to protest, it's only certain shit I can fight with her about because they are her kids at the end of the day. She complains that I spoil them too much, but I disagree. I guess that's probably because I don't have any kids of my own, and other than Micha, I'm not around any others.

The house ended up being the second of the two we picked because the first one sold before we could put in our bid. Monee was pretty disappointed but, in my opinion, there wasn't much of a difference. They were both five bedrooms, three-and-a-half bathrooms, with a dining area, sitting area, living room, finished full basement, and a full backyard. The only difference was the size of the garage and a fireplace. Monee claimed to want a fireplace so bad, but she wouldn't be the one cleaning it, so I was happy we didn't have one.

I'm happy that we are moving in like a family because I've never had one of my own. Growing up, it was always me and my niggas; they were the only family I had. Hence, that's why Rich and I are so close. Rich's mom is like my mom, and whether he's close to them or not, that's the only momma I've known.

Monee's kids aren't biologically mine, but I don't treat them as such. I know that shit gets under her baby dad's skin, but I don't give a fuck. Long as that nigga stay in his place, I'll keep the peace between us. The moment I feel like he's on some other shit with these kids, I'm going upside his head no questions asked. Eventually, Monee and I will have our own kids. I'm in no rush, so when the time is right, I know God will bless our union with a miniature me. I say miniature me because Monee already has a little her walking around here. Danee is the spitting image of her mom and D-Man looks just like his dad with very few traits from Monee.

Funny thing is, I made fun of Monee when she talked about having little events at our new house, but I couldn't wait for football season to start. Hosting game parties and just kicking it with my fam were days I looked forward to. As much as I used to enjoy kicking it at the clubs and running the streets, that shit was now so played out to me.

"Man, you won't believe what I just found out?" Rich bust into my office like he always does with some bullshit.

"Man, what? I'm sure it's some bullshit like always. You act like you ain't got no work to do. You just be bored." I said to Rich because he always found a reason not to be in his office behind the desk.

"Nah, real shit. Why the bitch Ceeda fucking around with DeWhite, Monee's baby dad. Small ass Columbus, right?" That shit got my attention quick. Cause I honestly thought he was just coming in there to talk shit and play around.

"Damn, fa real. Columbus is small but that bitch pussy hole big so it's no surprise to me that she got around to him, but damn, Monee's baby dad. I can see some shit coming from that. Long as they leave my household out of that bullshit, I'm good."

"Knowing Ceeda messy ass, she did it on some childish shit trying to get under Monee's skin just cause that's some childish shit she would do. Trying to get back at Monee for being with her man." Rich joked.

"Nigga, I was never her man. I smashed a couple of times, but shit, who ain't I hit that was willing to give it up. That shits all in the past. I'm not stunting that bitch, and Monee ain't stunting that nigga. As far as I'm concerned, they can go live happily ever after and never show their face around here ever again. It wouldn't mean me no never mind."

I was keeping it real; I didn't give a fuck about either of them two muthafuckas. I know for a fact Ceeda a hoe and DeWhite a poot butt ass nigga, so whatever they make of their situation, I wished them the best of luck.

MONEE

I don't know why out of all the people in the world Julian would reach out to me. That nigga knows I ain't like him when he was with my sister, so what in the hell would make him think I like his ass now. I may have gone through a phase where I wanted Monica to leave Rich, but even if she would have left him, it wouldn't be to get back with him. Shit, I'd rather her be cheated on than beat on any fucking day.

I thought it was a big ass joke when he emailed me the first time. My first question was how the hell he got my email address in the first place, then my second question was why. The initial email, I ignored but, after he started sending them on a daily basis saying how it was important for me to respond, I had to reply. I kept it real with him and told his ass Monica is happily married and I know for a fact her husband wouldn't approve of her reaching out to him.

Julian being half-retarded replied asking why did her husband have to find out. Like, what the fuck kind of drugs was he using to think my sister would risk her marriage for a nigga that wasn't worth shit while she was with him? I had to let his ass know to stop contacting me, and it was time to move on with his life because whatever he was trying to rekindle with my sister was long gone.

Of course, I told Kilo all about it, and his first response was not to get involved in that shit. He knew I wasn't because he knew the way I felt about Julian, but he made it clear to give his opinion on the situation. Kilo went as far as telling me that, if Julian reached out to me again, give him Kilo's number, so he could set him straight. I told him I would, but I was hoping like hell he didn't because if Kilo had to set him straight, that meant Rich would be involved as well; I hadn't even mentioned it to Monica. I didn't even want to bother her with that type of madness when her life was finally going good. Monica didn't have time for any more drama or stress from exes whether they were hers or Rich's.

It had been a couple of weeks since I sent the last message to him, and today, I got another email. I guess he just wasn't going to get the point. I was a little hesitant about opening the email because only Lord knows what that man had to say, but I knew ignoring him wouldn't do any justice. Clicking the email, I said a silent prayer that this fool would just get the point already, and I wouldn't have to say anything else to him, but just my luck, this prayer would go unanswered.

Monee, the only reason I am contacting you is because I can't get through to Monica. I don't know if she has me blocked or whatnot. I know you said she has a husband and moved on with her life, but I just need to speak with her. There are a few things I need to talk to her about. If need be, then I'll just take the next route and find where she works and go see her face to face. I'm trying to go about this the correct way, but you're leaving me no other choice but to do things on my own. I hope this message gets across to you, and you can set whatever difference we had aside just to pass my message along.

I had to read that message a good two or three times because this man was practically threatening me to show up at my sister's place of business if I didn't have her call him. I don't know what type of shit he was on, or what was so important that he needed to talk to her about, but this was the last straw. Before I tell Kilo about this, it's time I let Monica know what's going on just in case this foo gets on some other shit and really does show up somewhere. I don't want Monica to be caught by surprise because Julian doesn't have them all obviously.

Scrolling through my call log, I found Monica's number and waited for her to answer.

"Hey, sis!" Monica greeted me.

"What's up, boo? Quick question before I start my conversation, are you around Rich?" I questioned. I needed to get the story across to her first and allow her to decide if this was something she wanted to share with her husband or not. If Rich was around, I would just have to wait and tell her a little later.

"No, he just left to go meet Kilo at one of the shops. Why, what's going on?" Monica sounded like she was ready to hop on some bullshit. That's one thing I've noticed. Since her taking Rich back, she's always ready to go from zero to one hundred at the drop of a hat. If she even thinks he's up to no good, she's going apeshit. I find it funny because that was never Monica, but he really has brought another side out of her. I don't know if it's for the better or worse.

"Girl, it's nothing to do with Rich. I just wanted to tell you first. Just in case you didn't want him to know, I ain't need him all in our conversation like he normally is with his nosey ass.

"Oh, Lawd, what the hell is it then?"

"Ok, let me make this story as short as possible. Julian reached out to me via email a little minute ago trying to contact you, but I kept ignoring him at first. Then, the stupid asshole kept on sending me emails talking about how important it was for me to respond. I finally wrote his ass back and basically told him you moved on with your life and to stop writing me, but he ain't get the point. It had been a little minute, and I thought he would have left the idea of talking to you alone. I didn't want to bother you with the nonsense, because I know you're not thinking about him, but I received another email today, and he basically said that, if you didn't call him, he would come to find you, so he can talk to you about whatever it is he needed to. I didn't reply because I just read it, but I don't know what to say at this point. Like, I honestly don't want you reaching out to him, but we all know he ain't dealing with a full deck of cards and don't need him trying to blow down on you nowhere.

"What the hell is wrong with that man? I haven't talked to him in years. When I left him, I didn't talk to him back then when he would reach out to me, so what makes him think I have anything to talk to him about now. After all this time, what the hell could he possibly have to talk to me about? It's been years; we've never crossed paths, and we don't deal with the same circle of people, so what does he really want? If it wasn't for Julian being so hot-headed, I would ignore him, but knowing the type of person he is, that bitch nigga would really pop up out the blue and try to start some shit."

"I know, and that's exactly why I felt like I needed to tell you before shit got out of hand and it be too late to tell you."

"I don't even know what to say, honestly, cause I don't want to talk to the nigga, but I don't want him showing his face anywhere near me. I'm gonna have to tell Rich about this because I honestly don't know how to handle it."

"Yeah, that's the best thing for you to do. Let me know what Rich says after you talk to him. I'm bout to get this laundry finished before these kids have to be picked up. Call me if you need me, or I'll just call you once I'm done."

"Ok, I'm bout to call Rich and figure out how I'm going to handle this situation." Monica said before we ended the call.

I couldn't do anything besides shake my head because lawd knows I was at a loss for words for her. I already knew Rich was about to go the fuck off and want to know where Julian was located. I'm sure he is going to want to go see him and ain't no telling how that shit is going to play out. Thank goodness, I already told Kilo, cause it's about to be some shit and I don't need to hear his mouth about me keeping something like this from him.

The moment I hung up the phone with Monee, I sent Rich a text letting him know we needed to talk ASAP. I didn't know how or what I was about to tell him, but I was for sure about to let him know what was going on. Julian and I have a dark past, and I'm not trying to revisit it. It's not that I'm scared of him, but I'm not about to go through the motions of dealing with that nut case. That muthafucka used to beat the shit out of me and, once I got away with my life, I promised myself I would never go back. I refused to even talk to him after to get the rest of my belongings, so what makes him think I want to talk to his ass now? It's been a little over five years since I've been away from him. So much has changed during that time, and I thought he would have moved on by now. I guess he hasn't.

All the thoughts that are going through my head only caused me to have a fucking headache. It didn't help that Micha was crawling around the house pulling up on any and everything trying to walk, not allowing me a second of peace. I'm not complaining because I was loving every milestone she reached, but damn. Time has flown by so fast that baby girl will be one in less than two months. It seems like it was just yesterday that I found out I was pregnant and scared if I would be able to carry full term.

She's spoiled rotten and I'm not the only one to blame. Between Rich, Monee, and Kilo, that girl is going to be a damn diva before she's five. That's another reason I had to make sure to get this situation handled with Julian because I can't afford to be out in public and this foo approached me when I have my child with me. He didn't care about my safety, and I was the woman he claimed he loved, so I know he won't give two fucks about my baby. I may have never fought him back when it came to me but, over mines, I'll kill that man and I'm not trying to have to do all that.

"So how, you want me to handle this situation, babe?" Rich questioned me in a serious tone. I had just explained to him what Monee told me about Julian and all about my history with him.

"I don't know, babe. I just don't want to have to worry about him doing anything stupid or trying to hurt me or Micha." I honestly told him.

"That's one thing you ain't even gotta worry about. When it comes to you and my seed, won't nobody ever hurt y'all as long as I'm living. I can promise you that." Rich said, and I could see the lines form on his forehead as he finished his sentence. I could tell this matter was bothering him the moment I told him Julian was practically stalking me through my sister.

"The only thing I'm going to tell you is to handle this the best way you feel fit and be careful while doing it." I said before I stood to go prepare Micha's bath water. I'm not a killer but don't push me and, at this point, that's what I feel Julian has done.

"Say no more." Rich said before I heard him heading down the stairs, probably to his man cave to call Kilo like always. They say me and Monee are bad but the two of them are far worse than us. They talk on the phone more than we do any day.

Something told me I would need to take a couple of days off from work, so I sent out a text to the house managers. I let them know I wouldn't be in due to a family emergency. That's the joys of owning and operating your own business. You have the power to take off when necessary. We had enough staff at all the businesses to take days off when needed, and I'm thankful for that. All of our employees are trustworthy, and we don't have to worry about our business going to hell if we aren't there every day.

"Micha how, you get food all in your hair, pretty girl? Huh? Tell Mommy how you got food in your ponytails?" I questioned Micha as if she was really going to reply. I was washing her up and lathering the shampoo into her hair while she was giggling and playing in the bubbles. Moments like this I enjoyed. I wouldn't have it any other way. Being a mother has shown me another side of life that I was missing out on.

"Lean back, baby. Let mommy rinse the soap off so we can get out of here and get you in bed." Micha always hated the water being poured by her face. She would have a whole fit as if I was trying to drown her little self. After rinsing all the soap off her, I wrapped her little body in the towel and headed into my room to get her night clothes on.

Rich was in the room with all Micha's essentials sitting next to him on the bed. The diaper, Vaseline, lotion, baby moisturizer for her hair and her onesie night outfit.

"Babe give her to me; I'll take it from here. You can go ahead and take your shower and stuff now if you want to." Rich said reaching out to grab Micha from my arms.

"Thanks, babe." I said as I handed him the baby and turned towards the shower.

One thing I can say about Rich is he is a great father. I've never had to take on the task of doing anything on my own. He's been here every step of the way pulling his load as well. From making bottles to cleaning them, changing diapers throughout the night, and even staying up on the nights she was sick.

He said he wanted to have a few more, but I didn't want to have too many kids back to back. Besides, I still feared it may be complications with my pregnancies, so I wanted to take it slow. It's bad enough I'm already about to have baby number two. This pregnancy isn't even over yet, and he's already talking about baby number three and four. Although I did use to want a bunch of kids, I no longer feel the same way. I don't want to overwork my body nor my mental with a house full of kids running around on top of my other responsibilities.

We had been watching this careless ass nigga Julian now for a couple of weeks just trying to decide when the time was right for us to make our move, and tonight was the night. Julian lived in a little half a double at the end of his block. The opposite side of the duplex was empty so if we caught him going inside. No one would ever hear him begging for his life. The moment he pulled his key out to open his front door, we rushed up behind him and followed him inside.

I tried my hardest not to bust this nigga' head wide the fuck open, but the thought of him fucking with my woman and my sis caused me to hit him harder than I expected. Blood started pouring down the nigga's face instantly and, for a minute, I thought he had passed out, but it only dazed him for a second. He screamed just like the bitch I knew he was, and I low-key felt bad for his ass until Rich started talking and it reminded me why we were here to see him in the first place.

"Listen, nigga, I'm not gon' play with you like he did. I just need to let you know now one wrong answer and you sealing your own fate. So, I advise you to listen and listen closely. You understand?" Rich yelled at him.

"Yeah, man, whatever I need to do I'll do. I don't want any problems. I just got outta jail and I'm not trying to do anything to fuck up my life. I swear to God I'm not." This nigga sounded like a straight bitch, but I knew he was still trying to hold onto his manhood because he was giving us eye contact the entire time.

"Oh, trust me, I know you don't want these problems, but you barking up a tree you know nothing about. My sister-in-law tells me you've been trying to get in contact with my wife even after she told you to leave well enough alone. What's up with that?"

"It's not how it sounds. I swear to God I'm not trying to bother Monica's life. It's not what it seems, my man. I promise it was not directed toward you." The nigga actually sounded sincere.

"Oh, so you tell this man no disrespect, but you just totally accept the fact that Monee asked you to stop contacting her. You never once told her what it was about so how the fuck was, she supposed to take it?" I had to ask because he said he wasn't trying to disrespect Monica, but what about my woman, shit? She was the one he was blowing the fuck up for weeks at a time.

"Nah. Nah. Nah. I never came at her in any disrespectful way, either. I just really wanted her to pass the message alone. I swear yawl this is a big misunderstanding." As soon as he said that, Rich cocked his gun back and aimed it in Julian's direction.

"Nigga, you keep saying what it's not, but you're not telling us what it is. You don't have any reason to contact either one of them. So, the only misunderstanding I see is you not knowing when to let the fuck go and leave muthafuckas alone. Let her be happy. I mean ain't you did enough to her in the past. I should blow your brains out right now just on the strength of what you did back then." Rich was making himself even angrier thinking about what Monica had told him about her and Julian's history.

"No! No! No! I was trying to contact Monica to warn her. I wanted to warn her about somebody I know. I just recently pieced it together, and I don't know all the details, but I know he's out for bad. Although when she walked away, she hated me, I still don't want anything to happen to her, especially if I can prevent it. Monica doesn't deserve that. She's a good woman, and I know she couldn't have done anything too wrong to him."

"Wait, what you mean you wanted to warn her. So, what you trying to tell me is some nigga is after my wife, and he's trying to cause harm. You say you don't know the details, but you seem to know who he is and that it's my wife he wants to hurt. How do I know what you're saying is the truth? Who is he and why should I believe you?"

"I wouldn't lie. I just did two years in prison. I'm not trying to ever go back there. While locked up, I changed. I swear I did. I regret putting Monica through the shit I did. My right hand to God I do. I met him in the halfway house; his name is Keith. We got close, but I never knew who he was talking about when he would be talking, so I'm used to letting the shit he said go in one ear and out the other, but recently when I saw him, we had a few words. When I saw him, he was happy as hell to tell me he had finally found the wife of the nigga he had been trying to find and that he was going to make him pay through hurting.

He mentioned Monica's name, but he called her by her maiden name which is why I didn't even know she was married. Since it's her husband he really wants to hurt, I'm assuming that's you and its some bad blood y'all had from the past about his fiancé. Like I said, I don't remember all we used to talk about because I really thought he was just crazy, but you gotta believe me. Man, I swear you gotta believe me."

I don't know if it made sense to Rich, but the shit definitely sent off a light bulb in my head. All the shit that had been taking place lately was starting to make sense. The detectives are coming to get Rich and reopening the case after two years. Then, one of Monee and Monica establishments caught fire while they were inside. This nigga Keith really had it out for Rich, but he was gunning for everyone around him it seemed.

"Ok, so tell me what all you know about this Keith character and I'll let you live." Rich told Julian. Whether he told us or not, I felt like the nigga needed to die, but I was going to let Rich do the talking. We didn't need any more witnesses to come out the blue two more years from now and we all end up under the fucking jail.

"I don't know too much since we were released because we didn't keep in contact. He and I are from two different sides of town, and he's still in the streets and I'm not. The only thing I have on him now is his phone number and the address he stays at. I know he sometimes has his daughter so he's there on weeknights but other than that, I don't have anything. If I did, I would give it to you. My loyalty is with Monica as a mend to apologize for what I did in the past, not with him. Whatever comes to him he deserves. You ain't gotta worry about me ever."

PEW! PEW! PEW!

I sent three shots to his dome. Ain't no way in hell I was about to sit here and let this nigga lie talking about we ain't got to worry about him saying shit. Any time you will tell out of fear a man's whereabouts, to us I know he would've crumbled under the pressure of the police. He specifically said he wasn't trying to go back, so if that means snitching on us to protect his own ass, he would do it. I don't have time to risk those types of things when I can end it like I just did.

Rich gave me the side-eye and we both pulled the lighters out of our pockets. Prior to Julian coming home, we had already poured gasoline over the entire premises. Including the inside of the house. Julian was so scared the smell hadn't even bothered him. We dropped our lighters and headed out.

After dropping Rich off to his car, I headed home. That shit felt good to say. I had been heading to Monee's house for so long I no longer felt like I had a home and now we have one together; it's a different feeling. All these years I thought I didn't want a woman but I'm actually loving all the shit I was missing out on.

Chapter Four

MONICA, RICH, MONEE, DEWHITE, MONEE

Unlike my pregnancy with Micha, this pregnancy was going by pretty smoothly if you ask me. When I made my first appointment, I was in complete shock when the nurse informed me, I was already four-and-a-half months. My periods were all fucked up after I had Micha so missing a period wasn't something that was rare. I'm happy it's flying by because I can't stand being pregnant. The whole thing stresses me out.

I be scared about every single thing in fear of the baby's health. Then, Rich, Mr. Mom himself, is overprotective over the smallest shit. He won't even let me eat fish as often as I crave it in fear it's bad for the baby. I don't know what baby books his ass reads, but I wish he had left them wherever he found them.

Business is going well as usual. Since being pregnant, the only thing I really can do is go to work and home. I've been at work a lot more than normal. Supervision duties don't require much from me physically because I do most of the office work while Monee runs most of the field work. She hates being in the office, anyway, so it works out fine for us.

As of lately, we've been in the process of opening a daycare. We are only going to start out with this one first to see how it goes then go from there. Neither of us are really into the watching kid's ordeal, but since I'll have two real soon, and Rich is against putting them in child-care under anyone else, this is the best option for us. Besides Danee is about to start kindergarten, and since it's only half a day, Monee wants her to be in daycare the remainder of the day. The business should be a win-win for the both of our families if everything goes as planned.

We are scheduled to open next week. My baby shower is next week as well, so we got a busy schedule ahead of us. The ladies: Monee, Egypt, Princess, and Kina, were hosting the shower. As always, they do all my party planning. I can only hope the baby shower turns out half as dope as Micha's first birthday party did. I think they outdid themselves for that party. I was so pleased that I wish we could have made it a public event. Micha was so excited seeing Trolls everywhere. That girl loves her some Trolls. I'm a little disappointed that I'm having another girl, but Lord knows I probably wouldn't be able to handle a miniature Rich running around my house thinking he ran shit like his dad.

Rich is excited about having another daughter. He claims it's going to be easier raising girls compared to raising a little boy. His ass even had the nerve to fix his face and ask me could we have another one before this baby turns one. Of course, I declined. I've gained so much weight with this pregnancy I don't care if I ever get pregnant again. I feel like a fuckin whale. No matter how healthy I eat, I still gain weight. I exercise and everything, but I'm still growing inches by the day it seems. Rich claims he's not turned off by all the weight gain, but I don't believe him.

❀

"Why, you being so hard on yourself? You just had a beautiful baby shower, and we just opened another business. Hopefully, within the next month-and-a-half, you'll be having this baby cause I can't take any more of your emotions. You are driving me up the wall, Nica." Monee fussed at me. We were sitting on her couch having a talk, and I broke down crying like always. It seems like, if I'm not crying, I'm eating, and if I'm not doing either of them, I'm sleeping. I can't get my life together for shit. I'm only eight months, but I feel like I've been pregnant for the entire year.

"I'm happy, but I don't feel like my family is happy. I'm not being the mom I should because I'm always tired. Micha is still a baby herself, and she deserves more attention, but I can't give it to her right now. I'm worn out over everything. If I walk down the steps, I need to take a seat and build my energy back up. Cooking dinner is even a task for me now." I explained.

"Girl, Micha ain't worried about you half the time. We all know she's a daddy's girl and she loves her cartoons. You're a perfectly good mother. What do you expect to be able to do? Monica, you're fucking pregnant. That baby is sucking the life out of you." Monee said before taking a sip from her cup. I wished like hell I could drink right now. It had been far too long since I had a sip of liquor.

"Stop calling my damn daughter baby like she ain't got a name." I laughed in between tears

"Well, shit. Mia is sucking the life out of you. Is that better? We all know she got a name but until she gets here, it ain't going hurt to call her what she is and that's a baby." Monee joked.

"Then, on top of all that, I'm worried about my marriage, Nee. I feel like Rich and I are falling apart. We don't seem as close as we used to be. I don't want to accuse him of cheating because I don't have proof, and I don't want to go back to the shit I used to be on with checking all his shit. That drove me crazy. Every day I was looking and searching just to catch him and take him back. If I was to find out he's cheating again that shit might break me right about now." I was pouring my heart out and my sister really looked like she was lost in what I was talking about.

"Get the fuck outta here, Monica. Do you really think there's something going on? Or are you just being emotional?" Monee questioned me with a serious look on her face.

"I do, Nee. We have sex like once a month, and then, when we do, it's only for one round. Rich and I ain't been like this since he was cheating on me back in the day. I mean, I know I've gained weight, and he's probably not attracted to me like he used to be, but it's not my fault I'm carrying his daughter." I cried.

"If you don't have no proof, don't sit around stressing yourself out thinking he's cheating when you don't even know. So, what you've gained weight; that's what pregnant bitches do. If you stayed the same size, I would be concerned, not only for you but for the baby as well. My fault, I mean, Mia."

"I can't wait until this pregnancy is over. I'm trying to be grateful and happy with all that God has done for me and my family, but I can't help but think about the negative things going on as well."

"Girl, listen, I'm not going to tell you to go looking for shit because you've been there and done that. But I will say this, until he brings the proof to your doorstep or in your face, fuck that shit. You got a beautiful family that these bitches would die for. You're where you need and deserve to be so stop being so hard on yourself. Nica, if Rich is home with you every night and taking care of home, fuck those insecurities. Sex ain't everything. I mean, it means a lot, but sometimes relationships go through those phases. He ain't disrespecting you and doing shit foul in your face so leave it alone."

"You're right. I'm just going to pray about it and leave all this shit alone. Maybe I am overreacting."

"Now, take your ass home, take a hot shower, and relax. I think Rich and them are closing up early, so he'll be home early tonight. Cuddle up and watch a movie. That always makes me feel better." Monee suggested.

"Yeah, that might help just laying with him and relaxing. Micha is staying with Rich's mom tonight, so I don't have to worry about getting up with her early in the morning." I gathered my stuff and headed out the door.

RICH

It took a couple of months, but my life is finally going back to normal. Business is great, the police ain't been on my ass like they were, and my home life couldn't be better. I still had some unfinished business I needed to take care of as far as Keith was concerned. When the time is right, I'll take care of him. I didn't want to do anything until after Monica had Mia because she's always worrying about me being out late or not home with her. In order to catch Keith, I'm going to need to stake out a little, and Monica ain't allowing that right now.

Today is the day the doctor is going to induce Monica, so my second princess should be here before tonight. I couldn't ask for anything else. Monica has been a nervous wreck for the past week, and I'm happy this shit is about to be over. She was overthinking everything and worried like this was her first-time giving birth. I mean, I'm no woman, and I don't know what the shit feels like to bust my whole ass wide open, but I'm sure with the medicine they give it can't be as bad as she makes it seem.

Since the birth of Mia was scheduled, Monee along with all Monica's other friends were all at the hospital awaiting Baby Mia. Of course, Kilo came up there for my support. Kilo looks at my kids like they are his nieces, so he wouldn't have it any other way. My mom kept Micha and Monee's kids were with their dad. After getting all suited up and dressed in my blue hospital gear, we were ready to get the show on the road. Monica was crying before the procedure even started. I tried to comfort her as much as possible, but nothing was working.

I stayed by her side the entire time, from the spinal, to when the doctor pulled Mia out of Monica. Unlike the birth of Micha, she was given a C-section this time. I didn't know that's what was going to take place so now I understood her nervousness. They literally had to cut her open to take the baby out. I think I started sweating and damn near passed out just knowing what they were doing on the other side of the cover. When I heard my daughter let out a soft cry, I immediately let go of Monica's hand and went to grab her. The doctor cut her cord, cause I'm not for all that type of shit. I would've really passed out. It's one thing to see a person's blood in the streets, but it's a whole different situation to see my wife cut and bleeding. I don't know what it is, but I ain't with it. Mia came out looking just like her big sister. You would've thought it was the same baby because the resemblance was so close.

The only difference between Mia and Micha was Mia came out weighing damn near nine pounds. She was eight pounds and eleven ounces. I couldn't believe Monica was carrying that big ass baby. I see now why she couldn't push her out. That probably would've ripped my baby shit all the way up to her back. Shit, she had a hard enough time pushing out Micha, and she was only six pounds even. Mia was only seventeen inches long, which was only an inch longer than Micha at birth.

Mia ended up being released the day after she was born, but Monica had to stay at the hospital for an additional two days until her blood pressure went down. I felt sorry for my wife because she was going through the motions. She was sad as fuck that the baby got to go home before she could. I asked her if she wants me to stay at the hospital with her, but she declined so I brought the girls up to the hospital each day to spend time with her. Being at the house with the two girls alone was harder than I thought it would be, but I did the shit to the best of my ability.

Not only was I happy Monica was healthy enough to come home

but for the simple fact that I didn't know how much longer I could take care of both girls by myself twenty-four hours of the day. I didn't want to bother my mom or Monee for help, because they were my kids even though they both offered. Seeing how much work it was to take care of both girls, I made sure to be there to help Monica as much as I could outside of work. Just as I did when it was only Micha, I made sure to be just as helpful.

Being a father of two was starting to become easier and easier by the day. I now truly understand the meaning of multitasking. Monica took some time off from work, of course, for her six weeks, but that's almost over. I told her to take off as much time as she needed. It's not like she wasn't her own boss. I didn't take any time off. I just cut my time in half. I would go in for a few hours during the day once I knew Monica was up and started for the day with the girls.

When Monica does go back to work, both Mia and Micha will be going to the daycare center Monica opened before she had Mia. I'm comfortable with that because it's right next to the group home Monica owns, so she's not far, and the people she hired she knew personally. If it was up to me, Monica would be a stay-at-home mom, but she's not going for that. She swears I'm trying to take her independence from her when I'm really not. I just want her to be able to stay home and raise our girls.

Hopefully, the next time she gets pregnant, she will give up going into the office and just run the business from home. I'm still trying to convince her to have another baby. Not right now but soon. I don't want my kids to be far apart in age. I want them all to be back to back, so they can grow up close. I don't see why we shouldn't have more kids. We got the money, love, and space for them so why not. Shit, I'm trying to be like the black Brady Bunch.

MONEE

"This old ass bitch got the nerve to wanna go play bingo. Like, how the fuck old are we, trying to make me age before my damn time. I can understand if you said the casino but bingo? Bingo, hoe. Really?"

"What the hell is wrong with bingo? We used to play that shit all the time as kids so not only old people play it. What's the difference? Shit, gambling is gambling if you ask me; there's no difference." Monica defended her choice of ladies' night.

"We all dressed up and your ass really wants to go to a fucking bingo hall. Like, of all the things for us to do on a night where we have no damn kids. I'm not going to bingo; that's a waste of my time. Your ass can go fill in the cards with your ink dabber thingy all night by your damn self. I'm going to have me a drink and dance my night away. Shit, it's been so long since we've gone out anywhere, and I just wanna dance and let my hair down."

"I mean, I'm open to whatever, but nobody was coming up with anything, so I suggested bingo. I love bingo. I go once a week and I enjoy the shit. I don't see anything wrong with it. I mean, I may be a little overdressed but shit we overdressed for a bar too."

Monica's ass thought she was slick. Her ass was hooked to bingo and she didn't want Rich to catch her at a club. Going to bingo would be a win-win situation with her.

"Overdressed for a bar or not, I'd rather be there than a damn bingo hall. I told you, now let's go. Why, we still sitting here discussing it?" I said before grabbing my purse. It was damn near ten o'clock, and I didn't know what bingo hall was open this late, but I wasn't trying to find out.

Hell, I don't know who was aging quicker between my circle. Monica is the second to youngest but acts the damn oldest when it comes to sitting around in the house under Rich's ass. I mean, ain't nothing wrong with being up under your man, because I love being up under Kilo's funky ass as well but, when it's time to step out, that's exactly what I'm going to do. All of us have children, and Monica got two now. You would think she would want to get out and let her damn hair down. Shit, Mia is a month now, I'm sure she's not at her granny's thinking about her momma, so her momma needed to have fun for tonight cause, come tomorrow, it's back to being a mom.

Kina is the oldest, Egypt is a year younger, I'm the middle of the crew, then Monica and the youngest is Princess. We all are homebodies but when it's time to have a ladies' night we try to turn it up a notch or two. At least once a month, we try to link up and catch up on life since we really only talk via text here and there because of our busy lives.

If it hit one time, I'ma pipe her
If I hit it two times, then I like her
If I fuck three times. I'ma wife her
It ain't safe for the black or the white girls

Three drinks in, and we were all feeling it. Hell, we had only been there for about an hour and were all trying to feel the effects of our liquor before it got too late and we got sleepy. Monica started off being really reserved, but she even had her tail on the dance floor showing out. I knew for a fact she had to be drunk cause she hadn't drank much since having the baby. Her excuse was because, prior to having Micha, she had got carried away drinking when she was dealing with Rich and his cheating.

Egypt's ass hadn't stopped dancing since she walked in. I could tell she really needed this night out. Kina was being really reserved, surprisingly, cause normally one drink in and she's in rare form. Princess, on the other hand, was cutting the fuck up as always. I needed just one more drink and I was calling it quits as far as the alcohol was concerned.

"Can I have one more Crown Apple, with a splash of cranberry please?" I requested from the bartender.

"You sure that's all you want? Are we closing the tab?" She questioned in return.

"Yeah, you can close it; I'm done after this one." I said while laughing because I said that after my second drink.

"Ok, I got you. I'll be right back with your drink and card." She said as she turned to retrieve my order.

As I expected, that last drink got me out my hookup. Before you knew it, I was right beside Princess on the dance floor fucking it up not giving a fuck who saw me. Normally, I try to stick to my normal two steps but not tonight. My feet couldn't stay still. My ass was bouncing with every move I made. The DJ fucked up when he placed "Rake it Up" by Yo Gotti and Mike Will Made-It. My alter ego of a member of the twerk team came out. I was swinging the hell out of my twenty-six-inch ponytail with the feathered swoop bang.

Just as I went to swing my ponytail to the beat, I felt like the front of my bangs were being ripped from my scalp. I was caught off guard, cause I know for damn sure my girls ain't let no bitch run up on me. Besides, I don't have any beef. I'm too old to be fighting and carrying on. My first reaction was to jerk my head back and try to look whoever in the face that had my fucking bang in a tight ass grip.

"Who the fuck you think you are? Out here swinging this fucking Yakki like you single or some shit." Kilo said between gritted teeth.

I can't even lie, that shit scared the fuck out of me. I ain't know whether to respond or to punch his ass because I could feel my tracks lifting from my scalp in the front of my head. Granted, some of my hair was left out to cover the track, but it was still painful as fuck. My hairstyle was too fresh to be getting ripped out.

"Kilo, if you don't let go of my fucking bang before you rip my damn hair out." I responded to him in the calmest tone possible.

"I ain't letting go of shit until you carry your happy ass out this muthafuckin bar. In this bitch not expecting to see me acting single as fuck shaking your ass, shit.

"Ok, I'm leaving. Just let go of my damn bang. What, you want my whole front to be fucked up including my damn edges? Shit, Kilo, this fucking hurt. At least, loosen up your fucking grip. Embarrassing me in front of all these people."

"Nope, I ain't bout to do none of that. We are walking out this bitch together, just like this. You should've thought about everybody watching your hot ass when you were just dropping it like it was hot. Never know when or where I'm going to pop out. Should've been acting like you had some sense and you wouldn't have to worry about your thin ass edges in the first place."

It seemed like the more he spoke the tighter he got on my hair, so my best bet was to just shut the fuck up and walk my happy, drunk ass on out the club with him holding my damn bangs.

When I finally was able to lift my head, I noticed Rich had a hold of Monica's arm escorting her out and the others were following behind him. These niggas were really showing their ass tonight. I wonder who the fucking snitch was that called and told on us. I didn't even think it was that serious for them to come in here acting all foolish. Yeah, we were all drunk and dancing, but we weren't dancing on any random niggas. So, in my opinion, they were overreacting.

"Ok, babe, can you let go now? We are outside." I asked, sounding like some little ass kid.

"Hell, nah. I ain't letting go until we get to my truck." Kilo said still sounding all pissed off like he caught me out fucking another nigga or something.

"Babe, can I at least go get my stuff out of Egypt's truck then?" I really had to ask for his permission to go get my shit. This is just flat-out ridiculous.

"Yeah, and you better hurry the fuck up. Don't make me have to come over there and snatch you up again, Nee. I'm not bout to fucking play with your ass tonight."

"Ok, bae, Ok." I said, and he finally let go of my bang. I had a fucking pulse at the front of my head. I couldn't believe he had my hair that damn tight in his hand. I was walking as fast as I could in my heels in the direction of Egypt's Equinox.

"Why the hell y'all bitches ain't warn me when that crazy ass nigga walked in the fucking bar? That nigga bout snatched me bald, at the front of my hair at that."

"Shit, I honestly didn't see them until it was too late." Princess explained.

"I had just took a shot, and I couldn't get your fucking attention. You was too turned. I ain't want to make it look obvious that I was trying to get you, or he would've probably snatched my little edges, too. Shit, I need all the edges that I have left to stay right where they are." Egypt joked.

"Bitch, I'm sorry. I was in shock. I froze up like a bitch in a scary movie or some shit. I had never seen no shit like that. Them niggas came in that bitch like Batman and Robin to save the damn day." Kina said with wide-eyes. I couldn't help but laugh cause these hoes were drunk, and I knew damn well they couldn't save me. I don't even know why I asked. After grabbing my shit, I noticed Kilo's headlight coming in our direction.

"Alright, y'all. I hit y'all up in the morning." I said and started walking towards his truck before he got out and yanked my bangs again. I'm sure if he grabbed me like he did the first time they would fall out in the palms of his hands.

The entire ride home, I ain't say shit. I stared out the window while he talked shit to me like a damn kid. I could tell he had drinks cause the nigga was slurring. If he wasn't so mad, I probably would have laughed at his ass. He was really acting like he caught me in the act of something. It's cute, cause he's so jealous, but it's scary at the same time because he real life ain't give a fuck about security or anyone else trying to stop him. Come to think of it, security is probably who called and snitched on our asses. I got something for their asses next time we go to the fuckin hole in the wall bar.

"Get your ass out of the car. What, you still sitting there staring out the window like we ain't home?" Kilo said, taking me out of my thoughts.

"Honestly, babe, I ain't even realize we were here." I replied while grabbing my heels in my hand and the rest of my belongings.

Kilo opened the front door and powered off the alarm system with his keypad. I headed right in the direction of our bedroom because I was about to pass the fuck out before my liquor wore all the way off.

The moment I got all my clothes off and comfortable into the bed, Kilo came in, the room with another drink in his hand damn near staggering. My baby was fucked up, and it was funny seeing him so throwed. The nigga couldn't walk straight. I don't know what made him think he needed any more to drink. It's still early, too. Hell, I thought it was at least two o'clock in the morning, and it's only a quarter after one. I know for a fact his ass better get in the damn bed before it gets too late. I'm not trying to deal with his ass up all night drunk. Kilo can be something else when he drinks.

"Spread them legs. Don't just lay there; let me see that pussy. You was out there throwing that shit in all types of circles; let me see that shit now." Without a second thought, I removed the cover from my body and spread my legs wide the fuck open so he could get a clear sight of my neatly shaved, pretty pussy.

"Now, play with that shit how I like it." Kilo said in a drunken, seductive tone. I put my two fingers in my mouth to get them wet and immediately started rubbing my clit in a circular motion to get my juices flowing. When I felt my orgasm nearing, I used my other hand to play with the clit while I inserted two fingers from my other hand inside of me. I was causing pleasures to myself that I couldn't believe. I don't know if it was from the liquor or the excitement of him eagerly watching.

"Hell, yeah. Just like that babe. Stop biting your lip; let me hear you moan. What, you holding back for?" I hadn't even realized I was biting my bottom lip as hard as I was. I guess it was feeling so good and I was so into it, it was an automatic reaction.

"Daddy...ohhh daddy. I wanna feel you inside of me. Baby, come. Come here." I moaned out to him, and he placed his drink on the dresser and headed in my direction while removing his clothes with every step. The look in his eyes told me he was about to put a thrashing on this pussy tonight.

Kilo made it to the bed and wasted no time. He planted his face right in my pussy and began making figure eights on my clit like he had a point to prove. With every swift movement of his tongue, I felt my body jerk. He knew exactly how to work his tongue and take my body to different levels without much effort.

While sucking and licking on my clit, I could feel him insert two fingers into my pussy hole and two into my ass and begin to move his hand in and out. Before I could even actually realize what he was doing to my body, I felt my ears begin to ring and my body begin to heat up. My toes began to curl, legs stiffened, and the rest of my body was shaking. I had tears escaping my eyes, and my cum was pouring out of me.

Hearing Kilo sip and slurp up my juice intensified the moment. After slurping up as much of my juices as he could handle, for now, he lifted his head, and seeing my juices on his mustache and beard was a pretty sight to see. I reached for him and he leaned near, and I used my tongue to clean my juices off his face.

While I was licking and kissing all over his face, I felt him place his stiff dick inside of me, and my body began to melt all over again. There was something about feeling him inside of me that took me to places I had never been before. I don't care how many times we had sex or how long we've been fucking, I could never get tired of him pleasuring me.

"Whose pussy is this?" Kilo started talking that shit in my ear and I begin to fuck him back like he wanted. Whenever he started talking in my ear, I knew that's what he wanted.

"Daddy, it's yours. This pussy is all yours." I moaned in his ear before licking his earlobe.

"Oh, yeah. This shit belongs to me and only me, right?"

"Yes, daddy! Only you!" Although I was telling him what he wanted to hear, I meant that shit from, not only the bottom of my heart but the pit of my pussy as well.

"Don't let me catch you out there, showing your ass for the next nigga ever again. You hear me?" Kilo was making a point to let me know he didn't approve of what I was doing and that I would obey.

"Yes, daddy. It won't happen again." I was talking in the heat of the moment, and a part of me wanted to test him again just so he could put it on me like this the next time but then I remembered how hard he pulled my fucking hair.

"Make sure it doesn't. I'll kill you and the next muthafucka if I think either one of yawl even has a thought of my pussy going elsewhere. Do you understand me, Nee?"

"Yess, daddy!" I yelled as I felt him hitting my spot. I begin to cum, and I know the feeling hit him as well. Kilo slowed down stroking and planted a soft kiss on the nape of my neck. I knew that meant it was over. I was ok because I came more times than a few, and I was ready to drift off into my slumber for the night.

DEWHITE

Monee just don't know how bad she pissed me off when she decided to have our son's birthday party separately. I understand we are co-parenting but damn really. The only reason I found out he even had a party was because, when I met Monee to get the kids on Sunday for a few hours since Jr birthday was yesterday, my daughter was talking about not wanting any more cake. When I asked her why she said that she told me they ate too much cake at the party.

What type of mother has a whole birthday party and doesn't tell the father and he's in his kid's life. That's some childish ass shit if you ask me.

When I called Monee to say something about it, she got on the defense talking about, if she didn't ask me for anything, then it was none of my business. Like, what the fuck do you mean it's not my business. That's my whole fucking son... my first-born and my fucking junior. Anything about him is my business, especially when I'm present in his life. I could understand if I was a deadbeat dad, but I'm not. When I told her that, she threw in my face that she doesn't ask me for shit.

That's her fault she doesn't ask for anything. My kids have whatever they need at my house, and I know they have what they need at hers, but that's not the point. The point is I should be involved in whatever activities my son has. I'm sure her bitch ass boyfriend was there like he was their dad. Just knowing he was present, and I wasn't was pissing me off.

After arguing with Monee for about fifteen minutes about why and why I should not be included in shit she does, I left it alone. It was like beating a dead horse. She just wasn't getting where I was coming from. I for damn sure hope she doesn't plan on continuing this type of behavior because if so, it's gonna be a big ass problem. I believe that her nigga has a lot to do with her decisions, and maybe what I need to do is have a talk with him. From what I know he doesn't have any kids of his own, and maybe, that's why he's trying to be Superman to mine. Hell, we all got seeds inside of us; he better bust them off into some bitch and create his own cause those two belong to me.

"What is it that you want from me? If you don't want me, why do you keep pretending like you do? I mean, you've already made it clear that you want your weak ass baby mom back. The only thing is she doesn't want your weak ass. I guess yawl two weak bitches are made for each other. I'm sick of walking around this bitch on pins and needles in fear you are going to up and just say fuck me." Ceeda was nagging at the wrong fucking time. I wasn't trying to hear anything she was saying right now.

"Man, listen, now is not the time to be wanting to argue and talk shit. I'm not trying to hear that shit. All I asked was could you fucking call and see what time Dave and Busters close, so I could do something for my son for his birthday. When you wanted to act like you couldn't hear or that you were too busy, hell yeah I'mma catch a fucking attitude. You ain't doing shit else besides laying on your ass."

"Get the fuck outta here with that. I ain't doing shit else. I bring as much into this house as you do, and I technically don't even live here. Financially, I help you more than you ever help me, so why are you trying to throw me laying down today in my face. Yeah, I get it, you and your baby mom are going at it, but that has nothing to do with me, so don't come in here taking shit out on me." Ceeda swore whenever I got into it with Monee, I was trying to take something out on her, but I wasn't. She just seemed to always act stupid at the wrong times.

"So, what you bring money into this house. Shit, it's not like you work for it. You scam all day every day so it ain't your money, to begin with. You act like it's coming out of your bank account. Besides, I don't ask you for a damn thing. You choose to do shit around here like it's your place, so I allow you. What, you expect me to decline when it's what you wanna do?"

"You just avoided everything that I was saying about wanting to be with me at the beginning of our conversation. That's the shit I be talking about." I knew exactly where this shit was about to go. Like every other argument Ceeda and I had, she wanted to make things official and I wasn't trying to do that. Instead of arguing about it, I always avoided it and left that conversation alone. I knew it would turn into another argument because I wasn't going to tell her what she wanted to hear, but what she wanted to hear wasn't what I wanted to do.

"I ain't avoiding shit, but I don't have time to sit here going back and forward with you about some petty shit when I'm trying to take my kids somewhere to celebrate for his birthday. Now, either you going to shut the fuck up and come on, or you can stay your grumpy ass here." Enough was enough. My kids were sitting in the front room waiting for me, and I'm in the bedroom arguing with this bitch about nothing, wasting time. I only have them for a few hours, and I'm not about to take all that time arguing with Ceeda.

"Why wouldn't I go? You sound stupid. It's Jr's birthday, and I want to be a part of it just like I should be."

"Well, get your shoes on and come on. We are wasting time." I told her and grabbed my wallet off the dresser. I should've made her stupid ass pay for everything since she wanna throw up how much money she bringing in.

"Do you want me to call Keith and invite them since we are going to a kid place?" Ceeda asked. I hadn't even thought about Keith and his kids cause I was so pissed.

"Yeah, tell them we're going to the one out by Sawmill since that's closer." I told her which location to have them meet us at because there were two different Dave and Buster locations in Columbus. I didn't want them to be confused and show up at the wrong building.

The kids ran wild for about three hours straight until I was done swiping my card and Monee was blowing me up talking about it's a school night. I ignored her for the first half hour but when I realized she wasn't going to stop; I finally gave in and answered her call. Danee and Jr were having so much fun I didn't really care that it was a school night. She acts like they are in high school, and it would matter if they missed a day or went in late. If it wasn't for my kids saying they both wanted to go home tonight instead of staying with me I would've let them keep playing until the place closed.

Keith's daughters were running around having a good time with my kids. I noticed that whenever Keith came out to bring his girls to something, Ceeda always covered their tab. I wanted to ask what that was about, but I declined getting in his business. Keith seems like a coo dude from our first encounter at Chuck E Cheese until now; it's always been good vibes from him. He's a good father from what I see and always has his children. It's not too many of us good dads around nowadays.

Keith and I kicked it and shot pool together a few times but nothing more because I really don't go out often. Most weekends, I have my kids and during the week, I be too tired from working second shift. I don't wanna go anywhere. When I do step out to the bar or somewhere like such, I don't always wanna bring Ceeda with me, so I only see Keith whenever I'm with Ceeda. That's her brother, and I know his loyalty is with her. I don't need to be out and run into another bitch and he snitched on me. I know it's a guy code to keep a closed mouth, but I don't know how close they are or if he will run back first chance, he gets.

I dropped Ceeda off at her place and went to meet Monee to drop the kids to her. You won't believe we actually been meeting up to exchange the kids now for almost a fucking year. The only time we don't meet up is when she drops them off at my parents' house. She was really sticking with her word when she said she didn't want me knowing where she stayed at. It's not half as serious as she be making shit. I don't know what got into the woman I used to be with, but I can't stand her some days. She's starting to really play the bitter baby mom role. She acts like, since we aren't together anymore, we can't get along. She's even went as far as putting me on child support lately.

All chances of us getting back together seemed like they were out the window. I'm coo with it because the person she is now is not the woman I was once with. I can't be with no bitch who thinks she runs every damn thing and, in reality, the only thing she be running is her mouth. Her having a couple of businesses now and her money a little longer has gone to her head, I think. So, what, she owns a few companies; she still an average bitch if you ask me.

I used to think Monee was everything because she's so cold when it comes to her appearance, but that shit ain't even top-notch how it used to be. Her attitude is making her ugly. Monee stands a good 5'6 with shoulder-length hair that she used to only rock in a bob, but now, she be wearing all types of hairstyles and weaves. She's thick as fuck; I wouldn't consider her to be plus-sized nor skinny at a size sixteen, but she's got ass, hips, and tits for days.

Her stomach is even flat after two kids. As a matter of fact, her stomach went right back flat both times a week after she gave birth to our kids. I don't know how she preserved her figure, but she did. Her brown skin used to have a glow that would make you think she wore make-up but the only thing she ever used was Blistex. Again, something else she's changed up because now when I see her, she's got on lipstick matching whatever shade of clothes she has on.

The changes in Monee just go to show you a man can change a woman. She could be doing all this because it's the shit her man likes, but that only says he doesn't like her for who she is naturally.

"Took yawl long enough to get here. I told you I would meet you here in thirty minutes over an hour ago." Soon as I pulled up, Monee was talking shit.

"I'm not trying to hear that shit tonight, Monee. We are here; that's all that matters now." I replied.

"You gonna make it where I don't allow them to be with your ass on school nights if you can't respect my curfew for them." I squinted my eyes and looked at her sideways. Did she really just threaten me with my own fuckin kids?

"Get the fuck outta here. You can't give me a fuckin curfew with my damn kids. You can try if you want to. We wouldn't be going through these problems if you allowed me to just drop them off at home. I don't understand why it's such a big secret where yawl live. You act like I'm going to be popping up at your house and all types of childish shit. You can get it through your head, I don't want you. I just wanna be a father to these two; that's it, that's all."

"Nigga go the fuck on. Ain't nobody says you wanted me. Obviously, you still feeling some type of way about me to bring that up. If I don't want you to know where we live then you don't need to know. We have been doing this now for a year, and your ass should be used to it already."

"I'll never get used to it. You just keep doing little slick, spiteful shit to piss me off every chance you get. If you must know what took us so long, I had to take them out and celebrate his birthday since you had a party without inviting his dad."

"That boy is eight years old. Meaning, he's had a total of eight birthdays. If you hadn't mentioned a party to me or brought up the fact his birthday was coming up, I'm not about to call you and ask your input cause if you really cared, you would have addressed me about his birthday, but you didn't. It's over and done with, and my kids need to get home and in bed." I swear to God, if it wasn't for my kids being right there, I would've cussed Monee's childish ass out and probably smacked the fuck out of her for being so damn stupid.

"We going to have to go to court cause I'm tired of your fuckin mouth. Let's see how the judge feels about me paying child support, but you got a whole nigga who sells drugs for a living." I said, and she pulled off.

I know that last remark made her feel some type of way. I wanted my kids to hear it, too, because they have a dad who busts his ass every day the legal way, and Monee got them looking up to a thug thinking he's a good guy. I'll leave that conversation for her to have with them when they ask what it means to sell drugs for a living.

To come into the house and deal with Kilo's attitude after arguing with DeWhite over Kilo only pissed me off even more. This man doesn't understand that the world does not revolve around him. He called me twice while I was arguing with DeWhite, but I didn't answer because I didn't feel the need to explain to him why I was even arguing with that fuck nigga. Hell, I was already gone an extra fuckin hour longer than I needed to be, so I know that made him feel some type of way too.

I tried to call him back once I talked to my kids and explained to DJ what a drug dealer was, and that Kilo wasn't one. Soon as I pulled off, my son was asking questions. DeWhite knew what he was doing when he screamed like a little bitch. He's speaking on shit he knows nothing about because Kilo been gave up that street life.

The thing that pissed me off is that he wanted to get the courts involved. Child support is one thing, but to get a visiting schedule and all that was a whole other. He doesn't even have space at his house for my kids to stay with him. The nigga still stays in the same two-bedroom apartment he lived in when we first separated. Thinking about all of this only made me need to have a glass of wine. I told my kids to go shower and get in bed. Thank goodness, they are both very independent and know how to do those things themselves because I was about to explode if I didn't get something in my system and quickly. Kilo had one more fucking door to slam, and I was going to lose it.

The moment that thought crossed my mind, he slammed something in my room so fuckin hard it sounded like something broke. I grabbed the bottle and headed straight upstairs. This muthafucka had lost his damn mind.

"I don't know what the fuck is wrong with you or what your problem is, but right now is not the time for this shit, Kilo." I yelled as I walked into the room.

"You wanna know what my problem is, huh? Huh? You wanna know? You are my fucking problem." Kilo yelled back.

"I'm the fucking problem? Really? Me?" I asked.

"Yes, you!" Kilo replied.

"You can love me, or you can leave me. At this point, I'm really starting not to give a fuck. But what you not about to do is sit up here and play these childish ass games with me like we kids. I'm not going to force you to do anything you don't want to. If this ain't where you wanna be, then say that shit. You had more than enough time to make up your mind and decide if the family thing is what you really wanted. I know you don't have kids, and I understand that sometimes it can be a load, but when you got with me, you knew what it was.

I never sugar coated shit when it came to me and DeWhite. I always kept it one hundred with you. So, for you to sit up here and have a petty ass attitude over nothing and slamming shit is stupid. I can't control that man nor his behavior. The only thing I can do is make sure he's not disrespecting my kids, our house, or our relationship. I mean, what more do you really want from me at this point?"

I couldn't hold it in anymore. It seemed like, every time I had to go meet up with DeWhite to pick up or drop off my kids, Kilo would get in this funky ass mood. It's almost like he assumed that DeWhite and I had something going on when we don't. DeWhite is the furthest thing from my mind. I wouldn't fuck around with him even if the nigga paid me to do so. I'm over that part of my life, and I wish Kilo would get the shit through his thick ass skull.

"I ain't playing no childish ass games, and what the fuck you mean love you or leave you? You ain't going no fucking where, and neither am I. You and whatever nigga you thinking about leaving with will both end up in fucking body bags. Play with me if you want to. You assuming shit and yelling like I said something to your stupid ass. This my muthafuckin house, too, in case you forgot, so if I choose to slam some shit, then so be it; I'm going slam it."

"You saying I'm a problem, but I don't know where the fuck that's coming from. You say you ain't leaving and, neither am I, so what the fuck do you mean? Make up your fucking mind."

"What the fuck is that supposed to mean? Like I said, neither of us is going any fucking where." Kilo was really starting to piss me off talking in circles and shit.

"Listen, I'm not about to argue with you. Especially, while my fucking kids are here. You heard what the fuck I said, and you know you got a fuckin attitude, so don't try that denying shit with me. I'm not stupid nor blind. I've been with you long enough to know when something's wrong, and you've been pulling these little stunts for a little minute now, but I'm tired of it. If you feeling a certain way, speak on it instead of acting all childish like the fuck I said."

"For you not to want to argue, you sure do keep going on and on about nothing. I'm not going to argue with your ass whether the kids here or not over some shit you don't know what you're talking about. All I said is I'm sick of that bitch ass nigga DeWhite. I don't like the way yawl be meeting up or none of that shit. Now, you obviously feel guilty about something to come in here talking shit. It is what it is. That nigga is the father of your kids, and there's nothing I can do to change it, but if I find out there's anything going on between you and him, both your kids will be fatherless."

As bad as I wanted to tell him that would be doing both of us a favor, I didn't. All I wanted to do was pick up my kids, go home, and cuddle up until I fell asleep but, since that wasn't happening, I just sipped my wine and let him know what it really was.

"You're so worried about what's going on between DeWhite and me, and there's nothing there. I don't know what I gotta do to prove that shit to you. The nigga is pissed because I won't let him know where we stay and because I didn't invite him to the birthday party. I waited for him to meet me with my kids for damn near an hour and, when he pulled up, he wanted to argue and threaten to take me to court about his visitation and rights. Then, when I was about to pull off, he screamed some shit about you being a drug dealer, and I had to explain to my fuckin eight-year-old what a drug dealer is.

Then, turn around and assure him that his father was lying about you being one and that you own and operate several companies for your money. So, when I say now is not the time for you to come at me about some petty shit, please understand I really don't have it in me tonight to go at it with you about unnecessary bullshit, Kilo." Although I was still cussin, I lowered my tone, because I really didn't wanna argue with my man tonight. I just wanted to sip and sleep at this point.

"Fuck you mean this nigga yelling shit like that in front of the kids? That nigga doesn't know shit about me to speak on what the fuck I do. I try to stay out of yawl little baby dad, baby mom relationship, but that nigga pushing it throwing dirt on my name. That's the shit we are not going to do. DeWhite's going to make me come see about his ass sooner than later, and he just don't know it." Kilo fumed.

"Babe, can we just leave it alone for the night? I really don't wanna even think about this shit no more. Please, babe!" I tried to bargain.

"Yeah, I'mma leave it alone, but mark my word, I'mma fuck that nigga up. I promise you that." Kilo said before throwing himself onto the bed.

Chapter Five

MONICA, RICH, MONICA

The way I had been feeling lately was bout to cause me to pull my fucking hair out. I don't know if I'm going through post-partum still or what, but I have been in my feelings like crazy since I had Mia. I thought my emotions were bad when I was pregnant, but these mutherfuckas are even worse now. It doesn't help that I feel like my husband is rejecting me. He's not showing me the attention he used to, and that shit is taking a toll on me as well.

I originally sent a text message asking the girls to step out and have a drink with me but, when they all declined, I decided I was going with or without company. I needed a drink or four to calm my damn nerves. As bad as I didn't want to go back to my old way of drinking to settle my inner thoughts, I saw that coming if things didn't change here soon. Rich was somewhere with Kilo, so I'm assuming they would be out late as well. The last time I went out was with the ladies, and that was an epic fail so hopefully tonight ends differently.

I hadn't been at the bar for thirty minutes yet, and I was already on drink number three. I was taking them back quick cause I didn't want to be out too late. Just an hour or two, and I wanted to feel my drinks before I got ready to go. Rich had called me a few times, but I ignored all the calls because I really didn't feel like talking to him at the moment. He sent a text and that got ignored as well. Shit, he would be fine. There were plenty of times he didn't answer when I reached out to him. I'll call him when I get in the car. Right now, I just need to clear my mind and have some me time.

I knew the moment I locked eyes with Trent in the bar while getting my Long Island Iced Tea, that I wanted to feel him inside of me. The only thing about that was I didn't think it would be right here in the alley behind the bar. As he unzipped his pants and pulled out his ten-inch monster, my mouth began to water. It's crazy that, after all this time of knowing him, I had never craved him like this until now. I don't know if it's what I'm going through personally at home or the liquor but, either way, I want him in the worst way.

Trent grabbed me so forcefully and pushed me up against the building the moment that we got out of the spotlight. He started pulling my dress up and rammed his dick inside of my kitty without any warning. Thank God, my kitty was wet and juicy, or it would've been painful. The last time Rich and I had sex was well over a month ago, and I hadn't used any toys lately. While motioning in and out of me, he used his free hand to unbutton the top of my dress.

Trent kissing and sucking on my left breast was intensifying the moment even more. I used my hand to massage my right breast while he fucked me slowly and sucked the left. So, as I began to tighten my kitty walls around his dick, he pulled out and told me to bend over. I did as he told me and used the building as my support. Again, forcefully, he rammed his dick inside of my kitty but this time from behind. When I felt my hair being pulled and him stroking me harder, just like that we were both prematurely cumming. As bad as I wanted it to continue for at least a few more minutes, I knew we had to get back inside because he had people waiting for him.

I didn't want anything more from him other than that quick nut, and I hoped he didn't want anything more from me. What we both just did was completely out of character for me, but it felt damn good. Had I known Trent would dick me down the way he just did, I would've been gave him some of Miss Kitty. Since this was a one-time thing and never would happen again, I didn't give him my new number or even ask for his in exchange. It would be just like a one-night stand with a stranger in my mind.

My actions make me feel like a real thot, but I don't care at this moment. I needed to feel some sort of excitement to relieve the tension I had bottled inside. I don't know if he's single or not, but let's just hope his bitch isn't inside with the rest of the people he's with. Instead of walking inside the back door of the bar like we came out, I chose to walk back inside through the front and allow him to go back through the exit we came out of. I didn't need the attention of those who would be by the exit to be on me. I'm sure I smelled of sex because that few seconds of pleasure were extremely intense. More intense than I ever expected it to be.

"You weren't expecting to see me sitting out here waiting on you, now were you?" Rich questioned as I turned the corner to head back toward the bar. Of all the people in the world, I wasn't expecting to run smack dead into my husband. My heart dropped to my fuckin ass.

"What? What are you doing here?" I stuttered. I was busted, and there wasn't any way around it. I had just fucked Trent in the alley behind the bar and here Rich is sitting right in front of the bar waiting on me. I know I look guilty. Shit, there was no way he was going to fall for any type of lie, so I might as well head to my car and handle this mess like a woman in the privacy of my own home.

"I advise you get to trucking it to your muthafuckin car before I get out of mines and cause a fucking scene." Rich said through gritted teeth.

Instead of arguing with him, I rushed over to my car and prepared myself for how things were about to go at home. I'm thankful Monee has the girls but, then again, I may need to call her because ain't no telling how Rich is about to react once we are behind closed doors. He's never hit me before, but that doesn't mean he won't hit me after what I did tonight.

As of lately, I know he's probably thinking I lost my fucking mind. The last time I went to a bar, he drug me out by my arm, and now he's following me home because I was fucking behind the bar. I can only imagine how I look to him right about now. The entire ride home, I said prayers for protection, guidance, and forgiveness. God is the only person who could help this situation, and although when I did what I did I wasn't remorseful, I'm regretting it like hell now.

Rich beat me home, of course, and when I walked in; he was already sitting on the couch with a bottle of D'usse sitting in front of him. It looked as if he had already drunk half of it. His eyes were bloodshot red, and I could see the stress line on his forehead. A part of me wanted to go shower and talk to him later, but I knew there was no way he would let me walk past without saying something.

"Before you say anything, let me go ahead and give my side of the story so we can get this conversation out the way." I spoke up before he started yelling and shit. Once he started yelling, I knew he wasn't going to allow me to get another word in. Mentally, I had already prepared to lose him after I confessed.

"Nah, I don't even wanna hear your side of the story. I know what you did. I'm not stupid, Monica. I know exactly what happened, and I'm not about to sit here and let you lie to me. I watched you ignore my calls and text from across the bar. Then, I also watched your hot ass walk out the back with that nigga. As bad as I wanted to walk out behind y'all and blow his fuckin brains out, I couldn't. I knew I deserved whatever you did after all I did to you. Plus, the thought of killing him right then and there would risk losing my girls and ain't no man walking this earth worth me losing them.

I know you fucked him; I can tell by the way you were walking back to the front of the building. I also know you not stupid so you ain't suck that nigga dick. Not saying it's ok that you fucked him, cause it's not, but I know you wouldn't stoop that low and put your mouth on another nigga. As bad as I wanna break your fuckin jaw right now, I can't. I love you too much to put my hands on you, but that nigga. Yeah, that nigga, he going to feel it. Just know that." Rich said before taking the bottle to the head. I took that as my opportunity to get a few words out.

"Your right; I did fuck him. There's no excuse for what I did, but it wasn't on some get-back shit, I swear. I just feel like you no longer want me. Like, I don't feel beautiful anymore. You don't even touch me. Like, the most we do is kiss, and that's before we leave the house. Can you imagine how it feels to be turned down by your own fucking husband? The way he looked at me is the way you used to, and I just wanted to feel wanted, needed, and craved. Again, it's no excuse, and it's fucked up you had to see any of that. I would've never done it had I known you were there."

"Whether I'm there or not, you're my wife. You shouldn't have to have a babysitter to keep your legs closed. But you know what? Honestly, Monica, I just would rather you shut the fuck up cause nothing you say is going to change how I feel about it. It's done and over with. Now, leave it the fuck alone, please."

"I'll leave it alone for now, Rich, but eventually we will have to talk about it. I don't want this to go unaddressed and drive us to bad terms. In order to move forward, we have to come to some sort of terms. I love you, and I want to be with you, but like you've done in the past, I made a mistake."

I was feeling guilty at first, but the way Rich was talking to me was really rubbing me the wrong way, I felt like he was degrading me like some sort of slut or something. A part of me wanted to tell that nigga checkmate, but I didn't know if that would cause him to get up and fuck me up.

RICH

At any moment, I'm ready to blow a fuckin fuse. I love my wife, but the shit she pulled the other night I couldn't seem to get out of my mind. Yeah, I forgive her, because I've done more than enough shit to her over the years, but I can't forget it. Seeing my wife walk out the bar with another man did something to my soul. I'm out trying to handle business to make sure our family is safe, and that this nigga Keith is no longer a worry, and she out here doing some hoe shit.

After getting hip to the GPS shit when Monica used to check my whereabouts, I started checking hers. They say the accuser is always the offender, so I figured she was only so slick cause she was doing some shit. The same way I wouldn't answer her calls she checked my shit; I now do that to her. That's how we found out what bar they were at when they had ladies' night.

Most of the time, she's where I expect her to be so it's never a problem. I'm not saying I don't want her out and about, but I don't like my wife being in the bar scene with Keith still out here walking around. I don't know what he might be up to, and I'm not trying to have her in harm's way.

Monica, for the most part, is at home, work, bingo, or Monee's but, for some reason, she felt the need to step out to the bar and then did the shit alone. She's naïve of what's going on with the Keith situation, and I wanna keep it that way. Kilo hasn't told Monee, either, because we don't want them being scared, but that's another reason we don't want them running around club-hopping getting drunk being sloppy either. When they are sober, they are normally on their toes.

Monica proved my point when I said when she gets drinks in her system she gets sloppy, and that's why ever since, I haven't let her out my damn sight. I love my wife, Lord knows I do, cause I would've fucked her up by now if I didn't. On top of the love I have for her, I honestly think the fact that I'm a father now has made me more conscious of my decisions. I try to consider them in every move I make. If it's not for the better of Micha or Mia, then there's no purpose of doing it. I even stopped going out on the regular, and I never thought I would slow up on that shit. I'd rather lay up with my girls and watch corny ass movies or cartoons. Not having a father-figure really made me value being a father; it's plenty of times I was spared just so I could be here now with them so I'm going to treasure every moment.

Since I'm unsure of how much the heat is still on the streets from that shit with the detectives and Free's bullshit, I don't wanna make no moves that I'mma regret. They haven't been on my case, but I don't wanna be too sure because they still haven't caught any suspects. When you make a decision based on emotions and impulse you can be sloppy. Every other night, I'm dreaming about doing something to that nigga Trent.

As for my wife, I'm sometimey with her. One minute, I wanna lay under her and be how we were before I found out, then the next minute I don't wanna see her fucking face. It's not as bad as it was the first couple of days, but now, I see why she used to flip shit on me and act all bipolar when I was fucking around. It's like, one minute you're happy, then the next you're not.

It had been a little over two weeks since it happened, and we haven't talked bout it since. The only thing that keeps us afloat with me giving her the silent treatment is that we have kids we take care of. I'm able to communicate with her without being verbal. Call it some bitch shit or whatever you want but, until Monica apologizes for what she did, I'm not saying shit to her. So, what I already forgave her; she didn't need to know that until she admitted to her wrongs. Whenever I cheated or did something fucked up to her, I didn't have a problem saying sorry. Sometimes you gotta push that pride aside and do what's best.

Instead, Monica has just been walking around this bitch like she's not in the wrong. I don't know who or what got in her head, but she's obviously smelling her own ass. As bad as I wanted to talk to my nigga Kilo about it, the shit was flat-out embarrassing. I don't care how many times I did it to her, it felt like shit when it was done to me just this once. I know Kilo wouldn't judge me, but I'm not the type to share my relationship business with anyone when it comes to my wife. Now, if Monica was just a random bitch or a fuck, I wouldn't care, but she's far more than that.

"Rich, are you ready? I already dropped the girls off, and we only have like an hour to get on the road before it's crunch time. I'm sure the lines are about to be long as hell." Monica came in the house questioning me like I was going to reply. She's lucky we already had prior obligations to attend this basketball game, or I wouldn't have been going. I ain't have no problem holding the silence until further notice.

"I know you're not going to reply. I don't even know why I came in here talking. I just thought today would be different. I mean, we are going on a damn date without any communication. Yeah, this should be real interesting." Monica said under her breath and headed out the door. I followed behind her because I wasn't about to ride shotgun in her car like a bitch. I was driving my own shit, and she can hop on my passenger side.

The entire two-hour ride to Cleveland, we listened to music, and Monica scrolled her phone. Not a word between the two of us. Shit gets more and more awkward every day, cause I wanna say something to her. I mean, my wife is one of my best friends, and I hate the tension between us two. I know deep down in her heart she feels guilty and sorry as fuck, but I can't force anything. I was once in her shoes but now the tables are turned, and I can't take the heat.

I knew I was in the wrong, but my pride wouldn't let me apologize like I should have done in the first place. As bad as I wanted to apologize, I just couldn't. I feel like I need to say sorry in a different type of way. Because of the level, I fucked up, a traditional I'm sorry won't work.

Rich has barely spoken to me the last few weeks, and it was killing me inside. I wanted to make up the moment we started fighting but I just couldn't. He knew I was in the wrong just as well as I did, but I couldn't bring myself to tell him sorry for something he deserved. No matter how long I waited to get my revenge, that still didn't take back the fact he deserved it. Whether it was back then or now, karma has no expiration date.

If it wasn't for us purchasing the tickets to this game months ago, we probably would have never come. I'm shocked we came alone because we for sure were no source of entertainment for each other being all silent and shit. Rich loves the Cav's and I know he really wanted to see this game. Besides, it was something else to check off of our bucket list as a couple. The entire ride here, I thought about how I could break the silence between us. What married couple goes into public not speaking to each other. I can only imagine how stupid we might look to others. I knew that half-time of the game was coming, and since we were sitting in box office seats, we had a lot more privacy than I originally expected.

I went to grab Rich an ice-cold beer, and the moment I handed it to him, I stopped in front of him then dropped down to my knees. The look on his face was priceless. I know he was wondering what the hell I was doing or about to do, but he needed and deserved this surprise. I pulled his dick out as fast as I could without him trying to stop me. After kissing all over the head, I used my tongue to get the entire thing wet before taking his entire manhood into my mouth. While sucking Rich, I used my tongue to make circles on the part of his balls that I could reach. I needed to deliver some fire head. Something to show just how sorry I was. Licking up his shaft, I made sure to show every inch of his dick the same attention.

Getting up from my knees, I lifted my maxi dress and revealed my bare ass. While out getting his beer, I tossed my satin boy shorts in the trashcan of the ladies' room, because I knew I would no longer need them. Sitting on Rich's lap with my back planted against his chest, I started moving my hips in a circular motion. Starting off with small circles and next switching up my pattern, I felt him moving in the opposite direction as I was. Then, I suddenly stopped and began to bounce up and down while tightening my walls to increase the pleasure for the both of us. I bounced as hard as I could until I felt his body tense up, and he released all of his seeds inside of me. I continued to bounce until I felt his dick go limp inside of me. When I felt he was all the way soft, I slowly got off his lap and dropped back down to my knees.

Placing his manhood back in my mouth, I began to suck and lick until I could no longer taste my juices or his. I didn't have any napkins, so I needed to clean him off the best way I knew how before putting his dick back in his pants. After feeling like I had got every bit of evidence off of him, I stood to my feet. Pulling my dress down first, I didn't care if I got mine because my mission was to please him at this moment. I used my hands to place his dick back in his pants and fasten his belt as I leaned over and kissed his neck.

"I'm sorry, baby. I hope you can forgive me. I promise you it won't happen ever again! I love you and disrespecting you was never my intentions that night; it just happened." I whispered into his ear.

"I love your crazy ass, too. Of course, I forgive you. I just had to teach your ass a lesson. I see you learned. I damn sure wasn't expecting no apology like this, but I appreciate the fuck out of it." He replied and kissed my lips.

"So, do I have my husband back?" I asked with a smile on my face. It felt good to hear him speaking to me.

"What, you mean? You never lost your husband. I ain't going nowhere. I just wasn't going to say shit to you until you realized just what you had done. I'm over that shit, Monica. You know I love you girl." Rich said before planting a wet, juicy ass kiss on my lips.

In all honesty, after the stunt I pulled, I expected to lose my husband. I know Rich had put me through hell, but to get him back the way I did after all this time was low on my behalf. I mean, bottom of the barrel low. Although I had every reason to do what I did because of the way he was making me feel at home, it's still no excuse for me. Had it been him cheating again, we would be divorced without any second thought. I refused to go through the shit I did in the past years and two kids later.

I know it was a blow to his heart, pride, and ego cheating on Rich, but he was pretty forgiving. I'm thankful no one else knew about it because that would have only made matters worse. There's nothing like being embarrassed on top of being hurt. It's like throwing salt in an open wound.

Chapter Six

MONEE, TRENT, RICH, MONEE

had done everything lately to keep Kilo's black ass in the house, and nothing has worked. I swear, this nigga done started acting like he single or some shit. I don't wanna accuse him of doing something he's not, but all this late night staying out and shit is starting to get on my last nerves. Granted, he's home every night, coming in at midnight and later is not ok when you're in a relationship. Especially, when you don't work in the streets and you have a legit job that closes no later than seven in the evening.

First, I put some of baby Mia's Polyethylene Glycol powder in Kilo's food and drinks for like three days straight. That shit made him poop like crazy, but it ain't stop him from leaving. He started accusing me of putting stuff in his food, so I stopped. I will admit the first day or, so it was funny as fuck watching him run to the bathroom so often. Especially, when I know the reason for his constant shitting. Monica told me I was petty for doing so, but I felt like if he wanted to play with my mind, I was going to play with his bowels. It's not like I did it for too long, so it wouldn't cause any long-term damage or problems. I mean, they prescribed it for a baby to take daily so it can't be harmful.

When the shitting didn't work, I hid all his damn draws, so he would have to wash and take more time getting dressed, and hopefully, that would cause him to change his mind while waiting on laundry. When he started asking where his draws were, my excuse was he probably fucked them up with his diarrhea, and he only went out and got a bunch more. Then, he realized those disappeared too and he caught on. He hit the nail right on the head when he cussed me out about hiding his draws. I thought I did a good job by hiding them outside in the garage in a tote, but I guess he knew his woman far too well because, even without finding them, he knew what I did. Once I was busted, I put all his underwear back where they belonged and just hoped he would keep his black ass home more.

After the food trick and underwear shit didn't work, I tried Visine. I saw some shit on Facebook about Visine making muthafuckas pass out sleep, so I tried it. The first time I did it, I think I put too much in his drink, so I never tried it again. I scared my damn self. Kilo's ass was passed out within minutes and didn't wake up until the next afternoon. Thank goodness, he didn't suspect anything; he just blamed it on staying up late and getting up early back to back and needing to catch up on his rest. I agreed with him and threw the whole damn bottle of Visine in the fucking trash. I just wanted him home more, not to kill or poison him. I mean, I do still love the nigga.

If a man sees that his woman is craving and begging for his time or attention, he should correct that shit before the next man does. In my opinion, a woman's intuition is just as good as a damn psychic, so if a woman feels like her man is up to no good, then nine times out of ten, he's up to no good. I'm not saying he's cheating, but he ain't doing right staying out late.

My momma used to tell me and my sister ain't shit open late but White Castle and legs. I know for damn sure Kilo ain't staying out for no White Castle burgers, so legs are his only option. I'm trying my hardest to remain coo and not jump to conclusions because he will see a whole different side of me. If he thought Monica was doing stupid shit, he ain't seen nothing yet. Fuck around and end up without a dick or balls to use.

Before Kilo and I made it official, I told myself that my next relationship was either gonna be my last or my first homicide. I'm hoping he makes the right decisions, cause I ain't trying to catch a damn charge fooling with his big dick ass.

The fact that Kilo wasn't answering my calls had me kicking myself for staying in on a Saturday night. I still had some wine in the refrigerator, so I decided to Netflix and chill it was. Three glasses of wine and I was starting to feel like I had some liquor. That's the exact reason I normally don't fuck with wine, cause that shit hits you out of the blue. By the time I finished my fourth cup, I heard Kilo coming in the front door.

"Look who decided to finally come home." I said from the couch.

"Here we go. Don't start that mess, Monee. I told you I would be home as soon as I could. That didn't mean to blow my phone up until I got here. You knew I was coming home so I don't even know why you get all worked up and shit. It's not like we live separately anymore. At the end of the night, you know where I'm going to be." Kilo was talking, but I could smell the alcohol reaping from his pores sitting damn near three feet away from him.

"Yeah, whatever, Kilo." I said while standing up and walking my empty little bottle of wine to the kitchen. After throwing the Moscato bottle in the trash and placing my wine glass in the sink, I headed upstairs to my bedroom stumbling a little.

When Kilo noticed me stumbling some, he tried to come to my aid and help me, but we both damn near fell and landed on the steps. We both sat there for a second trying to figure out how the hell we both fell down. Kilo sat up on the step and pulled me onto his lap. I only had on a long nightshirt, so my pussy was exposed the moment I spread my legs to straddle him.

He started rubbing my clit, and my juices started flowing instantly. I forgot all about being mad at his drunk ass and started unfastening his jeans. He ripped my nightshirt off me and began to slide his hard dick inside of me. I begin to pounce on his dick like crazy. That wine had me showing my ass on the steps of our house. I had never fucked on the steps, but it was so much easier to bounce compared to the bed.

I didn't even care that my knees had begun to hit up against the wood because it was feeling way too good to stop. Kilo started pulling my hair and being all aggressive like I like it. When he started pulling my hair hard, it caused me to increase the arch in my back because of the position my head was in. It's almost like I could feel every inch of him in my guts making me want to bounce even harder, but I couldn't. I was already turned to the max on the dick; wasn't much more I could do. Without rising completely off his dick, I turned to face the opposite direction, so I could ride him reverse cowgirl. I grabbed my ankles and bounced until I felt the cream seep from inside of me.

After that scene on the steps, we both managed to make it to the bedroom without falling again, thankfully, because we were both intoxicated. The entire walk to the bedroom, we couldn't keep our hands off of each other. We were kissing and rubbing all on each other like one of those corny ass scenes from a movie. Sloppy ass kisses and everything. Had anyone been watching us, they would've for sure had a show to see.

The moment we walked into our bedroom; we were at it again. I got on the edge of the bed and assumed the position with the perfect arch, so Kilo could deliver the dick lashing I knew he was about to. Kilo knew what I wanted and started slapping my ass like I had bad behavior or something; that turned me on even more.

On all fours with him inside of me from the back, I felt my orgasm coming along. As bad as I wanted this to last, I know I was about to tap out real soon. Kilo and I had been fucking like animals since he walked in the front door, but the liquor was getting the best of me.

"Yes, daddy, right there." I moaned. I knew whenever I referred to Kilo as Daddy it, not only did something to his ego, but it made him go so much harder in the pussy.

"I know you don't think that's it." Kilo said to me as I reached my climax. My body went limp and I became super relaxed. My body was worn out, but my mind wanted more.

Kilo pulled his dick out and flipped me onto my back. Going down, he wasted no time using his tongue to lick my clit as if he was in a pussy eating contest. My body started squirming because everything was still sensitive from the orgasm I just had. Kilo knew that meant I was only about to explode again, so he put his thumb in my butt only making the pleasure ten times more intense. I felt him moving it in and out of my ass. As he sped up his pace, I couldn't help but fill his mouth with my juices.

Kilo started slurping on my cum as if he was dehydrated until there was no more. He scooted up and placed gentle kisses on my lips and then forced his tongue inside of my mouth. Of course, I French kiss my man back; it was only right. As I tasted my own juices, I felt him entering me, and the moment he was fully inside, I began to come again.

TRENT

What's a man to do when he just can't get a woman out of his system? This is the question that's been playing in my head since the night I ran into Monica at the bar. Seeing her out and about alone was the last thing I expected when I stepped out for the evening. I can't lie, seeing her was definitely great cause it had been quite some time. The last time we spoke, she informed me she was working things out with her husband and we couldn't communicate anymore. When she first told me that, I felt like it was a bunch of bullshit, of course, because when she left him, I just knew it was my opportunity. I guess they both had other plans.

I still try to keep up with her and make sure she's doing well by checking on her Facebook page and, from what I saw, she was doing good. When I saw she had two kids now, I was shocked because she had just had the first baby not long ago. Hell, I too had had a child since we last talked. My son and Monica's oldest daughter are only two months apart. My son is younger by only two months.

Beth is my son's mom; she and I are actually still together and doing good. Or should I say we were doing good up until I ran into Monica. I'm enjoying the family life. Taking trips, date nights, all that good shit, but running into Monica put a wrench in my plan. I never expected to cheat on Beth for Monica, but I did, and I can't take it back. I wouldn't take it back even if I could. It just happened and flowed so naturally. I felt like it was supposed to go down the way it did. Had Beth not been inside the bar, I probably would've followed Monica when she left. That one time wasn't enough; I felt like I owed her so much more.

I wanted to give Monica the deluxe dick down. When I say deluxe, I mean suck her pussy until she can't take it anymore, then eat her ass like never before. After I'm done giving it to her orally, I wanted to make love to her in every position possible until we both fell asleep in each other's arms. Even if we could only have one night like this, that would be more than what took place.

For weeks, I tried to push the thought of Monica to the back of my mind, but I can't. It seems like Beth and I are starting to bicker and fight over little shit that means nothing to me but pisses me off the most. Every time we fuss and fight, I think about, if she were Monica, would it be this way. I hate to compare the two because they are complete opposites in every way possible, but mentally, I can't help but to. I'm sure Monica and her husband have to be going through a rough patch as well because, if not, she wouldn't have dared cheated. It was a time when she knew he was doing her wrong and still wouldn't step out, so things had to be either over or close to it.

After basically stalking her Facebook for a month or so, I finally decided I needed to reach out to her and see why she ran off so fast that night. Or at least to exchange numbers so we could keep in contact. I mean, we already crossed the line, so it shouldn't matter if we kept in touch. I'm sure she misses the friend she had in me because I miss the friend I had in her.

I messaged her three times and all three messages went unanswered. I would've called through Facebook messenger if I wouldn't have thought I would look like a fucking creep randomly calling her off Facebook. I talk about dudes like that but here I was desperate enough to be one of those dudes over Monica.

It didn't help that Monica had some fire ass pussy. I mean, I knew it had to be good, but I wasn't expecting it to be as good as it was. Even though the condom, I felt everything I needed to, so I can only imagine how good she feels without it. She just doesn't know she got a gold mine between her legs. Prior to that night, I was ready to propose to Beth, but now, I'm reconsidering it. I'm not blaming it all on Monica, but she plays a major role in my reconsideration.

I had really considered just turning around and not going inside the building, but I figured I hadn't come all this way for nothing. I live on the opposite side of town, and the roses I sent with the phone number got me nowhere. Here I am looking like a scared high school kid nervous to walk up to a girl's front door because of her parents. The only difference was, I was sitting in the parking lot of the building Monica now owned waiting to go inside. I didn't know what to expect but it's too late now.

I grabbed my phone and the flowers off the passenger seat and headed towards the building. I wish I knew which car was hers, but I don't so inside I must go. Ain't no telling who all works here or will see me that could possibly know Beth but that's a risk I'm willing to take.

"Hello, Welcome to Comforting Arms; can I help you with something?" The receptionist greeted me.

"Hello, I'm actually looking for Monica. I believe she's the owner. Is she in today?" I asked.

"Yeah, have a sea. Just a second." The receptionist informed me and picked up the phone to call Monica I assumed. I heard her say a guy is here, but she didn't know the reason and I specifically asked for her.

"She will be out in just a second. She's finishing up a conference call." The receptionist informed me.

"Thanks!" I didn't know what else to say. A nigga was nervous and worried all at the same time. Nervous because I didn't know how she was going to react and worried because I had no business coming to her place of business with flowers not knowing her current relationship status.

"Would you like any refreshments while you wait?" The receptionist offered.

"No thanks, I'm fine." I declined.

"How can I." Monica greeted me but was caught off guard when she realized it was me, she was coming to meet. I stood to my feet and walked in her direction. "Trent? Trent, what are you doing here?" Monica questioned, and she unconsciously took the flowers I was handing her.

"I've been trying to reach you but you're a hard person to get in contact with. I wrote you several times on messenger then sent flowers with my number, but all went unanswered." I explained my reasoning for coming to her business.

"I'm flattered that you thought about me this much, but I can't accept these. Trent, I'm a married woman. You can't just be." She stopped talking right in the middle of her sentence and looked as if she had just seen a ghost standing behind me. I turned to look in the same direction and I saw Rich walking through the front doors of the building. The look on his face was as if he was the devil himself. He was walking so fast it's almost as if he was charging at me.

RICH

I thought my mind was playing a trick on me at first when I noticed Trent walk into Monica's building. I just so happen to be over at the daycare center dropping off the girls a box of diapers. I normally send the diapers with Monica but, since I was in the area, I thought why not run in to see my girls and drop off their weekly supply of diapers. Coming out the building, I noticed him sitting in his car looking all stupid, but I didn't expect to see him get out the car and head inside. I noticed he had flowers in his hand, and I assumed those were for my wife.

This nigga just wasn't going to stop until I stopped him from breathing. He got a sample and done lost his fucking mind. I don't know what they had going on, but this shit going to fuck around and make me kill both of them. Monica knows I'm not about to play about what's mine, so I don't know why she would even entertain this clown. If Trent didn't know about me, he was for sure about to learn. I sat in my car for a second thinking about my next move. I didn't have my piece with me, and it's a good thing because I probably would've shot his ass in the parking lot.

After waiting a few minutes and he didn't walk right out the building, I figured Monica was inside actually entertaining the nigga. If that ain't some disrespectful shit, I don't know what is. Everybody in the building knows Monica is a married woman and that I'm her husband. Why would she even allow him to come to her job knowing I could pop up at any time?

When I walked in the building, Monica locked eyes with me, and I saw fear written all over her face. I'm glad they were in the entrance way of the building, cause had they been in her office, I may have fucking lost it even more. When Trent turned around to see what had Monica's attention, he locked eyes with me as well and, before Monica could say another word, I socked that nigga right in his shit.

Right there in the middle of the lobby, I took off on him. I didn't care where I was at because he obviously didn't care that she was married. When my fist connected with his jaw, he stumbled back a little running into a display stand knocking everything on and by it down. I heard Monica scream for me to stop but I couldn't. Trent tried to defend himself, but I was too mad. I just kept swinging blows left and right trying to take his head off his shoulder. I felt someone pulling me off of him, but I blacked out.

By the time I was pulled off of Trent, there was a bloody mess in the lobby where he was laying. Monica was screaming and crying, and Kilo was the one holding me. He was pushing me out of the door, and I wondered where the hell he had come from.

"Bring your ass here!" I yelled at Monica. She was screaming and crying like she was hurt for the nigga. Although she looked terrified, she walked out of the building like I told her ass to.

"The fuck is wrong with you smiling in this nigga's face. What the fuck is he even doing here?" I yelled at Monica.

"Bro, this ain't the time or the place for this shit. Handle this shit at home. The receptionist called. Somebody called the police, bro. We don't need this type of heat right now." Kilo was trying to talk some sense into me, and I wasn't trying to hear him at the moment. I saw Trent's bloody ass face walking out of the building and rushing to his car. I didn't know if he was rushing to leave or to get something, so I tried to break away from Kilo to get at him again, but his grip was on me too tight.

"Brah, get the fuck in the car man. You kid's next door, this your wife's business, and you causing too much of a scene. This ain't you. Get in the fucking car and calm down. Handle this shit another time." Kilo was still trying his hardest to defuse the situation and pushing me into his truck. The only thing that made me actually listen to him was when he mentioned my kids. I could give a fuck less that this was Monica's business.

Kilo drove me home, and I was so pissed I hadn't realized we arrived. Monica called my phone a few times, but each call went to voicemail. I wasn't about to argue with her over the phone nor listen to her explain herself. I needed to see her face to face to determine if she was bullshitting or lying, and I couldn't determine that by just hearing her voice, especially since she was just crying. I couldn't come up with any other reason for her to cry other than her being guilty. Trent had no business at her job; it made me question if they had still been sneaking around or what. I'm her husband, and I'm the only man that should be bringing flowers to her at work or buying them period.

I may have slacked up with the way I used to spoil her and have little surprises, but that doesn't mean to get it from elsewhere. I try to do spontaneous things here and there, but it's different now that we have kids; that's not intentional, but it's just the way it is. Kilo pulled off as soon as I walked into the house, so it was only me alone to sort my thoughts until Monica brought her ass here. If she knew what was best, she would hurry the fuck up. Being so caught in the moment, I left my car at her building, but I would worry about that later. It's not like I planned on going anywhere anytime soon. It's still early and the kids won't be out of daycare until six.

I heard the alarm chime, letting me know that Monica had just walked into the house. A part of me was ready to take off on her ass just like I did Trent, but I decided just to keep my distance. If I don't, I'm going to fuck around and choke her dumb ass out in here. Might fuck around and kill my wife I'm so muthafuckin mad.

"Rich?" Monica called out. She probably didn't think I was home since there was no car outside.

"The fuck you yelling my name for?" I yelled in the direction I heard her tone coming from.

"I was trying to see where you were at." She replied in a defeated tone. I walked out of the dining room area and met her in the front room. Monica wouldn't walk far from the front door; my guess is she was going to make a run for it if I came too close to her.

"Why the fuck you still talking to the nigga? Why the fuck was he bringing you flowers to work? You still fucking that nigga, huh?" I barked questions to her.

"No. No. Babe. I swear to God I'm not fucking him. That only happened that one time. I haven't even talked to him since that night. We don't have each other's phone numbers or nothing. I swear, Babe!" I started crying as she was explaining herself.

"So why the fuck was he there? Why the fuck was you smiling all in his face taking flowers if you ain't talk to the nigga? Why you, ain't have your receptionist send him about his way then?" It just wasn't making sense to me.

"I don't know why he was there, honestly. Babe, you have to believe me! I didn't know who was there to see me. I had just walked out into the lobby not long before you walked in, and I was just telling him he couldn't do stuff like that out of respect for my marriage. As I was saying that, you walked in. Everything just happened so fast."

Monica had tears streaming down her face and, as bad as I wanted to believe her because she had never once lied to me, I couldn't piece together why a nigga would be bringing flowers to her job all comfortable and shit if they weren't in communication.

"You're telling him to respect your marriage, but you didn't when you gave him your married pussy. Oh, let me guess, you thought since it only happened once that would change his thoughts. The nigga saw that you were ready and willing once, so he going always think you willing."

"Rich, I know I fucked up, but that shit only happened once. You can't throw that in my face like I'm out here just fuckin any and everybody. When you cheated, I didn't constantly remind you or throw it up in your face, so why are you doing this to me? I dealt with far more than I have ever put you through. I can't believe you would throw this up in my face like everything is my fault. I've never once thrown up how many nights you would fuck that bitch Free then come home to me like nothing happened. Or, how when you finally decided to cut her off, she tried to fucking kill me. Never, Rich. Never have I.

I've given my all to this marriage and, no matter what I did that night, I've tried to show you that I sincerely apologize from the bottom of my heart. It happened, and I can't take it back. Other than that, one time, I've been nothing but good to you, so don't do this to me."

She was screaming and crying. As mad as I was, she was telling the truth. Monica never threw shit in my face, but I didn't know what else to say at the moment. When you're mad shit flies out your mouth before thinking about it. Although everything I said was the truth, I didn't mean for it to come out the way it did.

"I'm just trying to figure out why he was there, Monica. Why were you crying? You act like you were protecting him or something." I said. That was the only real reason I blew up the way I did. The look in Monica's eyes screamed busted whether she was, or she wasn't.

"Rich, I told you I don't know why he came. I haven't talked to him. Either, you're going to trust and believe me, or you're not. I've never lied, and I'm not about to start now. I have no reason but to be one hundred percent honest with you. You have access to all my shit. You can look through my phone, my Facebook, my email, whatever. You will see I haven't talked to him. Shit, if you want to ask the receptionist, she will tell you just how everything happened before you walked in.

I wasn't protecting him. I could care less what you did to him, but not at my place of business. I had families there and everything. Someone called the cops, another resident threatened to move out. Do you know how bad that looks on me? All because you jumped the gun and assumed something that wasn't even really what it appeared to be."

Damn, was all I thought to myself. At the end of the day, I didn't care where I was, but the business she runs has to do with the livelihood of my kids and that hadn't crossed my mind. Monica worked hard for her business and to get where she is today. I don't wanna be the reason she loses it, but my anger got the best of me.

"Look, Monica, I apologize for losing my temper at your job. I would never want to get you in any situations that would harm your business. But what I'm not going to apologize for is what I did or who I did it to. This ain't the last time this nigga Trent gotta worry about seeing me because this shit is far from over. I'm going to believe what you are saying this time, but make sure that shit never happens again on your end. Do I make myself clear?" I yelled.

"That's not a problem. It's no issue for me not to speak to or deal with him. Just promise me you will never do something so reckless like that without considering our family again."

"I promise you that." I gave her my word I wouldn't recklessly behave and jeopardize my family again over a nigga, but I wasn't sure if I could keep that word if I see him in her face again. I'm going to try my hardest to control my rage, but I want this nigga Trent dead."

Chapter Seven

KILO, DEWHITE, KILO, MONEE

ately, my nigga had been buggin out and doing some off the wall shit I had never seen before. I've known Rich damn near all my life, and never have I witnessed him spazz out the way he has been. Little shit been causing him to fly off the handle, and normally, he's the one who can contain himself. He's the one who has to calm me down most of the time, but not anymore. They say love will make you do some crazy things, and I'm witnessing that shit first-hand. I mean, I know Monee got me acting all types of different, but this nigga Rich not giving a fuck about anything.

The day the receptionist called Monee about Rich fighting at their business, I was confused as fuck. Luckily, I was right up the street from there, so I was able to get there in enough time to stop him before he killed that foo Trent with his bare hands, but I was lost as to what the fuck was going on.

Rich had just recently told me about Monica stepping out on him with Trent, so I knew why he was whooping his ass, but I ain't know what Trent was doing at the job. As bad as I wanted to question why he was there, it wasn't my place. I knew Monee would hear bout it and come to me wanting to gossip cause that's what females do. I'm not saying she be gossiping badly about her sister or anything, but my woman pillow talks with me. She tells me all their little females' business and problems. I like it sometimes, because I feel like she is being open with me and leaving no room for secrets but, other times, I don't be giving a fuck.

Females sometimes talk about and stress about the most stupid shit. Half the arguments she be telling me her friends have with their niggas be petty. Then, I have to sit back and think like, damn, do our shit really be that petty and pointless, cause it doesn't seem that way when it's me or Monee in the hot seat.

Back to Rich, though, that's my brother and I can't fault him for loving his wife the way he does, cause at the end of the day, she's not just some jump-off; that's really his wife. The woman he went to the altar with and committed to spending the rest of his life with. They vowed to the death of them, and I see that shit going that far, cause it's obvious at this point neither of them are going to leave the other one alone.

I'm not the most perfect nigga, nor am I saying I'm the best boyfriend to Monee, but I never said I was nor did I ever portray to be anything that I'm not. This is my first real relationship and, if you ask me, I'm doing a damn good job. I know I have a fucked-up mouth and sometimes come across as not giving a fuck, but I care more than a little bit for Monee and those kids. I also know that I have a hard time expressing my feelings when it comes to certain shit, but in my defense, I've never had to express my emotions to anyone outside of anger. With all those things counting against me in the boyfriend category, one thing I can say is I'm loyal. Not only to my relationship with Monee but to her kids as well.

It seems like, every time Monee wants to have a heart to heart and talk about our feelings towards each other, I'm at a loss for words and don't know what to say. I'm blank-minded and I'm sure she knows that. Sometimes, she says it seems like I lack feelings, but I try to show her through my actions that it's all there. Monee also complains about wanting me to be more affectionate. If you ask me, I thought I was overly affectionate. I give her dick every chance I get, and we cuddle every night. There's not a night that goes by she's not sleep in my arms or I'm spooning her, so I was lost on exactly what she meant by me needing to be more affectionate.

I'm learning more and more each day about this relationship ordeal. I swear, it's always something new. As long as Monee is willing to work with me and allow me to get used to things, we will be fine. We have been official for over a year, and I see us being forever. I can't see myself making steps forward like I have or risk I do for any other female ever in life. Every time I think of my relationship with Monee, I think of *Teach Me How to Love* by Musiq Soulchild.

҉

"*I*f you two foo's don't get the hell out of my kitchen while we are here trying to finish up, I'm going to starve both you muthafuckas." My OG ain't play no games about Rich and me being in the kitchen sampling shit while she's still cooking.

Rich's momma is the only momma I've known since I was a teenager. So, I call her my OG because that's exactly what she is. She took me in as if I was her own without ever asking where I came from or who I belonged to. Ma always used to cook Sunday dinners. No matter what other day out the week she didn't cook, she made sure to have us a hot meal every Sunday. Rich and I used to make it our business to be there faithfully each and every Sunday until Rich married Monica, then we started eating at his crib every week. Now that I'm with Monee, ain't no need for me to be at his crib when my woman cooks just as good as Monica if not better.

Ma ain't the friendliest woman to get along with cause her mouth is so slick, but we were able to get the ladies over here and help her cook Sunday dinner for us all. This was actually the first time all of us came together and had dinner. Rich, Monica, Micha, and Baby Mia were there. I brought Monee, Danee, and D-Man along with me. I'm excited about us all being together like a big ass family. Rich is technically the only child. Well, he was until I came around, so this big family thing is all new.

"I don't know how yawl two crazy girls got with these two crazy ass boys of mine, but shit, if y'all like it, I love it." Ma said.

"The only crazy one I see here is you!" I replied in our defense.

"You batshit crazy if you thought I was the only crazy fucka in this room. I witnessed far too much in my years to accept that I'm the only one crazy. Half the shit y'all go through and do I never thought of doing in my entire fucking life."

"Ma, you's a damn lie." Rich chimed in.

"Ya daddies the damn lie." Was her rebuttal.

"Fuck that nigga!" Rich said with laughter. Ma talked a lot of shit, but she knew the life we lived in the past and now, and she also knew that we wasn't no suckas when it came to the streets and handling our own.

As we all sat down and prepared to eat dinner, I noticed Monee give Monica a side-eye. I'm sure it was because of something Ma don said slick to one of them, and Monee was probably ready to let Ma have it. Out of respect for Rich, Monica stayed away from Ma unless it was to drop the girls off because they had exchanged words when Rich and Monica first got married. I just hoped whatever it was Monee wanted to say she could hold until we got in the car. The last thing I wanted was for Ma and Monee to get into it because I knew the filter levels my woman had, and I know just how ignorant my OG can get. The two most important ladies in my life can't go at it because I wouldn't know whose side to pick.

"Rich, did I tell you that Shauna came over here last week asking for your number saying she needed to talk to you about something important." I knew it was coming. We just couldn't get through the night without there being some drama. I wanted to laugh, but I knew my brah was in the hot seat and probably ready to kick Ma under the table to shut her the fuck up.

"Nah," Rich said and put a forkful of food in his mouth.

"Where the hell did she come from? Was this her first time coming over here looking for Rich cause I ain't heard about her in over two years." Monica asked.

"She don came by a few times, but normally, I don't open the door. This time she caught me as I was walking in the house."

"Oh, has she? This is the first I've heard anything about this."

Monica said and looked in Rich's direction. Ma knew this conversation could've waited until later when the ladies weren't present.

"Shit, it's the first I've heard about it, too." Rich said and gave Ma a death stare.

"What does it matter? I ain't give her your number, that's all that matters, but if she keeps on coming around her, I'mma tell her ass she needs to take that up with his wife because I'm tired of her coming around here like you live with me or something. Got me ducking her like a Jehovah Witness back in the day."

"That's fine; I'll talk to her with no problem." Monica said before taking another bite of her food.

By the time we got home, the kids were in the back seat passed out. Monee had a slight attitude riding home at first until I asked what happened between my OG and her. I already knew that's what it was because she would've come out and said something otherwise. Come to find out, Ma had the nerve to ask how long did Monee think we were going to last cause I'm not a one-woman man. That comment caught me off guard. Although that was true in the past, that wasn't her place to ask those types of questions.

I assured Monee that we were going to last until death and that I would be callin my OG as soon as we got to the house. If it was one thing I was going to address, it was the level of respect she had to have for my woman. I'm not going to allow Monee to disrespect her, so I'm not going to allow her to be disrespectful towards Monee. It's only right they are treated equally.

I knew it was only my OG's way of trying Monee just like she had with Monica, but that's not acceptable. I'm gonna nip those problems in the bud now, so they don't resurface later. After I promised Monee, I would handle it, she seemed to lighten up a little bit. I'm sure Rich's ride home was similar because of what was said about Shauna. Monica wasn't about to play that shit when it came to Shauna and her kids, especially now that she and Rich have kids of their own. She used to sit back and not say much, but those days were long gone.

I can damn near bet my last dollar that I wouldn't be going to Kilo's momma house for the holidays. That old bitch had me ready to punch her right in her fucking mouth. She just didn't know how pissed off she made me. Saying little slick shit about my relationship is one thing, but basically praying on our downfall is another. It's bad enough she left a bad taste in my mouth a couple years back when she got into it with my sister over the area her and Rich chose to move after they got married.

Like, bitch, if you don't go sit your old ass down somewhere and get you a man to tend to. I honestly feel like she doesn't want Rich or Kilo with anyone, so she can have them all to herself like she used to have. What she fails to realize is that they are both grown ass men, and eventually, they were both going to find someone and move on with their lives. Don't no bitch want no nigga who still sucking on his momma titty in they thirties. If that's the case, he can go fuck his momma and have her suck his balls.

I didn't expect Kilo to cuss her ass out about it, though. When I told him, I was only telling him because he asked what my attitude was about, I wasn't telling him for him to go check her because I'm all for keeping the peace between families. When I told Kilo that I wanted to keep the peace, his response was we are his family and ain't no peace if she starts chaos in his household. Everything he said was right, so I sat back and listened to him check the hoe. Yes, I called his momma a hoe cause that bitch tried me. Thank goodness Kilo wasn't no weak ass nigga that was scared to correct his momma when she was in the wrong cause that would have for sure put an end to this relationship.

When I called and told Monica how bad Kilo went off on that lady, she started cussing Rich out. I guess she felt that, if Rich put her in her place like Kilo had just done, then she would stop being so messy. You would have thought that their mom would have learned her lesson about Monica after she stood up to her back in the day. Maybe since her approach is different now, she thought Monica wouldn't say anything. She had another thing coming if she thought Monica wasn't going to speak up. She had been through enough bullshit with Rich than to let anybody come sideways at their relationship. I had to explain to Monica that her level of messy at the age she is, probably will never change. The only difference is she won't say shit directly to me anymore; it will all be sneak dissing.

I don't give a fuck what it is, as long as I don't have to hear it. It's not like I gotta be up in her face no way. Kilo and I don't have kids together, so she can talk all the shit she wants behind my back. That's his momma, not mine.

Since the kids had this Friday as well Monday off from school, DeWhite asked could he keep them the entire weekend. Like any mother, in their right mind, I didn't have a problem with it because that gave me some free time, as well as alone time with Kilo. Granted, DeWhite does normally get the kids on a bi-weekly, sometimes, weekly basis, I have them the majority of the time. I'm not saying I dislike having my kids, but every real mother knows what it's like to want or need a break.

When we met up for DeWhite to get the kids, I made it clear to his ass that he needed to meet me no later than noon on Sunday, because I would need to do Danee's hair for the week and also make sure their homework was completed. If we waited until six o'clock which was our normal meet-up time, I wouldn't have enough time to wash, blow dry, and braid her hair on top of helping them with homework. Danee got too much hair to try to do a rush job on, and I'm not trusting any female that he dates in my baby's hair. Just my luck, she would fuck around and come home bald-headed.

While the kids were gone, I planned on taking the time to clean the house and fuck my man as much as possible. Sounds pretty cliché, but that's the shit I enjoyed doing in my free time. The weekends are also my time off, so I don't have to worry about going in. Kilo and Rich alternate weekends, so Kilo's off as well.

I told Kilo's ass that I wanted to spend some alone time today and the entire time I was cleaning he was lounging around. When I finally got done and was prepared to just chill, this nigga had the nerve to actually be getting prepared to head out. It confused the fuck out of me why he waited until damn near ten o'clock to be leaving the house. I was trying my hardest not to argue with him because we were alone all weekend, and I wanted some quality time without any disagreements, but I see that wasn't about to happen. When I asked him where he was going, he told me to handle business. Handling business sounded like bullshit to me. His business was closed, and I'll be damned if his black ass was back hustling.

"You could've handled business earlier today while I was cleaning, and you choose to get ready and run out of here as I'm getting done when you know I wanted some alone time with you tonight." I fussed as he was getting dressed.

"Monee hush your damn mouth sometimes. I'll be back, damn. The kids are gone all weekend. You act like I'm not coming home tonight or something. We got all day tomorrow to lay up." Kilo argued.

"That's not the point. The point is I wanted to lay up tonight, tomorrow, and whenever the fuck else I decided to. You been lounging around all damn day, like, what the fuck?"

"Cause what I had to do I couldn't take care of earlier. If you don't go sit your ass down somewhere and stop getting all worked up, you bout to piss me off with this shit."

"I don't care about pissing you off, Kilo. I'm pissed so we will be even." It wasn't that I was mad; I was just being a brat. I hate when Kilo leaves. We could be with each other twenty-four seven and I still would want more time. When you love a person the way I love him, all the time in the world still isn't enough. We bicker and fight, but that's my heart for real. I've never felt this way about anyone the way I feel about Kilo and I think he knows that and uses it to his advantage.

"Whatever, Monee!" Was all he said in reply to me. I grabbed my robe and headed towards our bathroom. I was just going to take my shower and try to get some rest since that's the only option I had for tonight now.

Slamming the bathroom door, I heard him say something under his breath, but I couldn't make out exactly what he said because of the vents running when I turned the lights on. I turned the shower on and adjusted the water to my liking before undressing and getting in. Looking in the mirror, I pinned my hair up and placed the shower cap on so I wouldn't ruin my eighty-dollar silk press.

As soon as I got ready to lock the bathroom door, Kilo pushed it open, shoved me against the wall, and got on his knees. When he pulled my oversized shirt up exposing my neatly waxed pussy, I knew it was about to go down. He started kissing my thighs slowly while he used his fingers to toy around with my clit first. Seconds later, he was using his finger to spread my lips as he moved his tongue up and down.

I gently placed my right foot on his shoulder and allowed him to take my mind to another place. The feeling of him moving his tongue in circles around my clit was amazing. One thing about Kilo, he didn't eat the box often but, when he did, it was always nothing short of amazing. I felt my knees getting weak and, right as he used his fingers to penetrate me while still licking my clit, I felt my left leg about to give out as I started cumming.

"You good now; go ahead and take that ass to bed." Kilo said as he got up from his knees and kissed my lips. When I smacked my lips, he slapped me on the ass before wiping my juices off his face and heading downstairs. He knew originally, I didn't want him to leave me and that's the only reason he did that. Although I was still pouting, I was for sure about to take my ass to bed. I needed that nut, and I didn't give a fuck where he went any longer; he still had my scent on his lips so I'm sure there wouldn't be anything funny going on tonight while he was gone.

After being on my feet all damn day, I hoped that Ceeda had at least cooked something or cleaned up the place. Doing the overtime on my days off was killing me, but I needed to pull in some extra money to move. Since it was a wrap for Monee and me getting back together, I needed to get a bigger place before I took her to court for joint custody of my kids. I had everything else going in my favor, besides the space for my kids to actually live with me part-time.

Monee thought I was only throwing idle threats, cause I hadn't said a word about actually going to court since that night we argued, but I wasn't. I just needed to make sure all my ducks were in order before I made a fool of myself going to the judge. Monee can kiss my ass and that's on everything that I love. I'm not about to keep going through this shit with her.

When I talked to my kids about the argument we had in front of them that night, they basically told me that their mom told them I was a liar and I would say anything to turn them against her boyfriend, which wasn't true. I was telling the truth. The nigga is a thug and what type of woman allows her kids to be around thugs? She was putting our kids in harm's way by even allowing them to live in the same house as him. At any given moment, something could go wrong and then what?

When I walked into the house, it was quiet as fuck. I already knew Jr was on the game. I'm sure that's where he's been since I left earlier today. Knowing him, he's probably only moved to pee and eat, nothing else. Normally, Danee is in the living room playing with her dolls, but I didn't see her. I noticed the dolls were still on the floor, but she wasn't in there. It's still early for them to be sleeping, so she's probably in the room with Jr since Ceeda's lazy ass is stretched out on the couch sleeping. No dinner cooked or nothing. The place wasn't even clean. That's the least she could've done. She ordered fucking Pizza Hut again for the second night straight. I know my kids prefer pizza over anything, but damn, what about me? I'm sick of pizza, hot wings, subs, and all of that shit.

I walked into the back room to check on Jr and look for Danee, and Jr was in the same place right in front of the TV as I expected.

"What's up, Jr? You been in front of this TV all day haven't you.?"

"No sir, only for a few hours. Miss Ceeda told me I had to let the game cool off earlier, so I gave it a break." Jr replied.

"Oh, ok, where's your sister at?" I questioned.

"She's in the front room with the girls and Miss Ceeda." Jr replied without taking his eyes off the TV.

"What girls? Ain't nobody in the front room but Ceeda." I looked at my son awkwardly.

"Mr. Keith's kids." He replied as if that was a stupid question to ask him.

I walked out of my room and to the bathroom, but no Danee. Then, I went to the kitchen, but still no Danee. My place wasn't but so big, so she didn't have anywhere she could hide. I called out Danee's name and she didn't answer so I immediately went to wake Ceeda up.

"Ceeda, Ceeda, get up. Where is Danee?" I questioned her as she rubbed her eyes and frowned up her face.

"What do you mean where is she?" Ceeda questioned me back.

"Where the fuck is my daughter? She's not in here nowhere." I yelled.

"Huh? She was just right..." Ceeda said as she sat up and looked in the direction of Danee's toys but there was no Danee. "She was right here playing with Sabrina and Kenitha when I laid here because I had a headache. I'm sure Keith just came to pick them up and didn't want to wake me up.

"Nothing against your brother or anything, but you know how I feel about people being at my place when I'm not here. Why were they even over here? You didn't call and ask me or anything." I said to her. I was honestly a little relieved because I knew my daughter wasn't missing but damn.

"I didn't think it was that serious. I mean, you act like you don't know him. He's been over here before, and it wasn't a problem. You act like Keith is going to steal something from you." Ceeda had the nerve to catch an attitude, and she was in the wrong.

"Yeah, I was home last time; he came over here but today I wasn't so he shouldn't have been here."

"Look, I only called because Danee was bored playing by herself, and I didn't feel good, so I called and asked Keith to bring the girls over. It's not like I have a car to take them anywhere, so I did what I thought was best." Ceeda justified her reasoning for going against my orders when it came to my place.

"Ok, well call Keith and let him know to bring Danee back or that I'm on the way to pick her up. Monee would have a fucking fit if she knew my daughter went somewhere with somebody and she's never met them." I said shaking my head.

"How the fuck can she get mad. You know Keith, and she's your daughter, too. It's not like she's in harm's way. You know Keith, and Danee's been around him plenty of times. Who cares who Monee doesn't know personally? I'm sure she has your kids around people you don't know all the time."

"That's just how Monee is. Can you just get him on the phone, so I can go get Danee? I'm tired and I planned on coming in and relaxing, not coming in looking for my daughter." No matter what I said, Ceeda wasn't going to see anything wrong with the situation.

"I'll call him, but you're probably going to have to go get her, because I just had to loan him some money earlier cause he was low on funds, so I know he probably doesn't have any gas."

"That's coo; I'll go get her." I said as I headed to the bathroom to go piss because I had been holding my pee since I walked into the front door. Ceeda was calling Keith on speakerphone, but I could hear it going to voicemail. She called at least four times, and each time, the voicemail picked up.

"His phone keeps going to voicemail; it must be dead. Give it a little minute, and I'll call back. Let his phone charge up some."

"Alright." I replied, cause there was really nothing else I could say.

"Did you eat, babe?" Ceeda asked.

"Nah, I came straight in and woke you up when I didn't see Danee."

"I'm about to hop in the shower and eat something. Hopefully, he calls you back by the time I get done. If he does call back while I'm in the shower, you're gonna have to go get her."

"That's fine. I don't have a problem with going to get her." Ceeda said as she walked into the kitchen to make me a plate while I hopped in the shower.

"Aye, Jr. it's time to get off that game and head to the front room son." I yelled into my room.

"Yes, sir!" He replied, and I heard him powering off the game from the hallway.

"Ceeda, can you put on the firestick for him, so he can watch a movie?" I needed Jr to go lay it down before he started asking questions about his little sister. Jr knew the shit his mom allowed and didn't allow, and he would for sure tell that Danee was gone with Keith. That's the last thing I needed to hear Monee's mouth about.

Hours had passed and Jr and Ceeda fell asleep, but still no word from Keith. I'm trying my hardest to remain calm and not jump to conclusions, but the nigga could've called. I don't know how he is about his kids, but I don't just allow my six-year-old daughter to be gone with another man without making contact with me. Come to think about it, I don't believe Danee has ever stayed at anyone's house other than with me and my family outside of her mom's family. Certain things Monee just didn't go for, and I've respected her decisions up until this point. It was out of my control that Danee left with Keith in the first place, but I thought Ceeda would have enough sense not to allow my child to leave without my permission. It was bad enough I left them alone with her, and Monee didn't know about it.

As tired as I was, I couldn't get any rest. Every time I would drift off, I would wake back up and call Keith or check my missed calls to see if he had returned any of my messages. When I looked at the clock and realized it was damn near four in the morning, I figured I wouldn't be hearing from Keith until well after nine, so it was best I just got some rest in the meantime.

Waking up, I heard Ceeda in the kitchen cooking. She must've really felt bad cause like I said before, her lazy ass never cooks. I hoped she didn't wake Jr up with all the noise she was making because he would for sure start asking questions. I grabbed my phone to see if I had any missed calls from Keith and there were none, but I had one from Monee. I'm sure she just wanted to check on the kids or something, but I needed to see if Ceeda talked to Keith first before returning her call.

"Good morning!" Ceeda greeted me as I walked into the kitchen area.

"Good morning. Have you talked to your brother yet? I need to go get Danee. Monee called me while I was sleeping, and I'm sure she probably wants to talk to the kids. I'm not trying to hear her mouth about Danee not being with me." I said in a groggy tone.

"No, I called twice, and his phone is still going to voicemail. I hope everything is ok." Ceeda tried to whisper the last part under her breath but I heard her.

"What, you mean you hope everything is ok? It's not ok because he took my daughter for one without my permission. Secondly, he's not answering any call nor returning them. Whenever you have someone else's child, the number one thing you always do is keep in contact with the other parent, especially if that parent never knew you were taking that child to begin with." I had started yelling before I even knew it. Just thinking about how careless Ceeda was with my kids pissed me off. It's one thing for me to be careless but another for her to be.

"Calm down; why are you yelling and shit? You act like I knew he was going to not be answering his phone." Ceeda said in her defense.

"From the looks of things when I walked in, you didn't even know she was gone so how would you know anything? When you're supervising another person's kids, you're supposed to actually watch them and not your damn eyelids. Anything could have happened while you were sleeping, and you wouldn't have known because you didn't even realize she was gone in the first place." I was fuming.

"I'm sure his phone just died and that's it. But if it makes you feel any better, I'll go over to his mom's house. Nine times out of ten, that's where they are and probably still sleep. It's still early, DeWhite."

"Eleven ain't early. And yes, it would make me feel better if you went to pick her up." I said and walked out of the kitchen. The food she was cooking smelled good, but I lost my fuckin appetite.

I gave my keys to Ceeda and went back to lay down until she got back, or Jr woke up, whichever came first. I would worry about calling Monee back after Ceeda got back with my daughter. This was the first time Keith had ever taken Danee, but this would be the last. He's not even responsible enough to keep his phone charged; I'll be damned if I let her stay the night over there again. Now, his girls are welcome to come over here, but the other way around ain't happening.

I heard my keys hit the dresser and woke up. I hadn't even realized I drifted off. I grabbed my phone to check the time and it was damn near one o'clock in the afternoon. Another missed call from Monee and a text with her telling me to call her. I hopped out of bed to go talk to the kids and finally eat. Ceeda was sitting on the couch beside Jr watching TV.

"Where's Danee?" I questioned after searching the front room with my eyes.

"Umm, they weren't there. His mom said she hasn't seen him since yesterday morning." Ceeda nervously replied.

"What the fuck you mean they weren't there? You have been gone almost two hours and you came back without my fucking daughter.

Where the fuck are they then? You said he doesn't have his own place and, if his mom ain't seen him since yesterday morning, where did they stay last night?"

"I… I… I don't know. That's what took so long. I went to a couple other relatives' houses to see if he was over any of them, but he wasn't." Ceeda looked like she was scared at this point because she didn't know what my next reaction was going to be.

"I'm calling the police; this shit is ridiculous. I leave to go to work thinking my kids would be in good hands and come home and can't find one. The only thing your dumb ass can tell me is that she with your brother, but you don't know where he is or how to even get in contact with him.

"You can't file a missing person report until it's been twenty-four hours. I called before you woke up because I'm honestly worried. This isn't like Keith to disappear with his kids and not make contact with at least his mom." Ceeda said.

"Man, what the fuck!" I yelled while rubbing my hand on my head. "What the hell am I supposed to tell Monee?" Just as I asked that question, she was calling again.

"Hello?"

"I have been calling your phone all day. Where, my babies?"

"My fault; I'm out at the store grabbing a few things right now. They are with my mom." I lied as I walked to the bedroom so Jr wouldn't hear me talking on the phone to his moms and bust me out.

"Oh, ok. Well, have them call me when you get back. Monica wants to take the kids to some Disney on Ice thing that she just found out about. I wanted to see if they wanted to go or not. I know DJ might not want to go but Danee loves Princesses, so she might want to."

"I'll call you when I get back to the house." I said.

"Ok, make sure you do, so I can let her know before it's too late." Monee said, and I ended the call.

"This is the shit I'm talking about. This nigga got his kids in harm's way and don't even give a fuck. I love them kids like they my own. I hope and pray Monee don't know shit about this nigga having these babies around that snake ass nigga. If it wasn't for them kids being with him right now, it would be the end of this the fuck boy's life. This shit got me real-life fuming." I fussed to Rich. I couldn't believe that DeWhite would allow his daughter to be out with Keith without him present.

"My question is where the fuck is DeWhite? That nigga got to be plum dumb for letting his pretty ass daughter out his sight. I would never allow my girls nowhere with another nigga besides you. You can't trust these clowns around little girls nowadays, even if they do have kids. I know Ceeda had to be the way they met. Ain't no other way Keith would even have access to DeWhite.

Do Danee even know Keith like that? I mean, either way, Monee's kids shouldn't be around Ceeda or Keith, but still, is she familiar with him? Nigga, you better call Monee and let her know the shit that's going on with her kids. Tell her to call that nigga now and go get them, kids. I'm sure Keith knows who DeWhite kids belong to. Ain't no telling what type of plans he got or tricks he could be trying to pull. I don't trust that nigga or Ceeda. She's probably in on whatever plan he got." Rich was going off now, too. He considers Monee's kids to be his niece and nephew, so he was feeling some type of way as well.

"I'm bout to call her now. Go ahead and pull off. We are going to have to catch them both after Monee gets the kids. I'd rather be safe than sorry. I don't want them involved nor caught in any crossfire." Rich nodded his head at my remarks and pulled off as I dialed Monee's number.

Soon as Monee answered the phone, I got low-key nervous cause I ain't know how to tell her that her baby girl was in the care of Free's baby's dad. Which is the same nigga behind trying to take our family down. I hadn't even told her that we killed Julian and found out about Keith being behind everything because some shit she just didn't need to know until it was completely handled. I didn't want to put any fear in her, and I knew that's exactly what was going to happen once I told her about Danee.

"Hey, Love!" Monee greeted me sounding sleepy as hell. I'm sure she was probably sleeping because when I left, she was about to shower and get in bed. Knowing her she probably fell asleep reading her kindle.

"Babe, call DeWhite up and go get the kids now. Don't ask no questions, just do it." I demanded.

"But, babe, it's almost midnight. The kids are probably in bed sleeping. His ass might not even answer the phone. He took them somewhere earlier today instead of them going to Disney on Ice with Monica, so I know they all probably wore out." That's the shit I hated about Monee. Sometimes, she just doesn't know how to shut the fuck up and listen.

"Man, listen to what the fuck I'm telling you. Call DeWhite and go get them fucking kids." I said and hung up in her face. Not even a minute later, she was calling me back.

"Babe, he's not answering. What do you want me to do now? I told you they would probably be sleeping." Monee sounded as if she had an attitude, but I was trying my hardest not to alarm her. She was leaving me no other choice.

"Listen, I just saw the nigga Keith, Free's baby dad. Danee ain't sleep or with her dad; she's with him. So, what I'm telling you is get in contact with that nigga and go get them. I don't trust that nigga Keith. I'm out here trying to handle something and can't cause I see baby girl with him. This shit not sitting well with me."

"What?" Monica yelled. "What do you mean Keith has my fucking daughter? She doesn't know that man, and where is my son? Better yet, where is DeWhite's ass. I'mma call you back. I'm bout to call him again while I throw on something. I'm going over there. You sure that was Danee you saw?" Monee sounded as if she was confused and pissed off all at the same time. I know she was because she had no idea that Ceeda and DeWhite were even fucking around probably. I'm not even sure if she knows who Ceeda is or her connection to Free. Me and Monee never talked about it, so if she did know, she had never said a word to me.

"I know what the fuck Danee look like. I have only been around for how long? Call me soon as you get to his spot or send me the address when you hang up, and I'll meet you over there."

"Ok, I'll send the address now." Monee said and hung up the phone.

My nerves were getting the best of me because something in the pit of my stomach told me that nigga Keith was up to no good. DeWhite was foul as hell on so many levels to even let this type of shit go down without Monee's approval.

I got a text alert from Monee with the address. I knew the area DeWhite lived in, so I directed Rich on how to get there. Since we were on the opposite side of town, I'm sure Monee would beat us but, as long as I got there before she left, that was fine by me.

When we pulled up, I noticed Monee's car parked still running. She must've hopped out the car and ran inside. I tried calling her phone, but she didn't answer. When I got out of the car to head towards the door, I heard yelling and saw her coming out the house with D-Man by the arm. Had he not been so big, she probably wouldn't have been practically dragging him by the arm but instead carrying him but that little dude is big as fuck for his age. There was no way she could carry his big ass the distance from the door to her car.

"What's up? Where's Danee?" I asked her.

"This bitch ass nigga's going to tell me he doesn't know where she is. Then, when I asked why and who the fuck she was with, he told me she was with his fuckin mom. Going to tell me a bold face lie until I called his momma and that old bitch said she didn't know what the fuck DeWhite was talking about; she ain't seen the kids. DJ told me Danee's been gone since yesterday with some man named Keith. Finally, DeWhite decides to tell me he didn't want to tell me cause he knew I would overreact. That's my fucking daughter, and I don't know that man. He could be doing anything to my fucking baby." Monee screamed as she was putting D-Man in the car. The tear coming down her face let me know that not only was she mad but scared as well. Seeing my woman like that made me see red.

"Get him home. I'mma handle this. I'll call you in a minute. Make sure you answer the phone." I said as I gave her a kiss on the lips and wiped away her tears with my hand.

"Kilo go get my baby. Please go get my baby." Monee pleaded. She didn't even have to say no more because that was my plan.

"Don't worry, baby. I'm going to get her. Love you and text my phone when you get home. Rich already called Monica. She's on the way to the house, so she should be there by the time you get back."

"Ok, I love you, too." Monee replied before getting into her car and pulling off.

After I watched Monee pull off, I told Rich to come with me and head inside of DeWhite's apartment. The nigga wasn't living bad, but he damn sure wasn't living good enough to be giving Monee grief about taking the kids from her or joint custody. If the judge saw the little shack, he was calling a home, he wouldn't grant that shit no way.

DeWhite looked as if he was a deer in headlights when he opened the door to my face. I didn't even wait for him to invite me in. I pushed past him, and Rich followed. He tried to leave the door open, but Rich immediately advised his ass to close and lock it. The nigga did what he was told without any second thoughts. To my surprise, Ceeda was sitting on the couch looking all scared. She just ought to be scared cause she had parts in this little dumb ass setup, to begin with, and I know that for a fact.

"So, I'm not about to waste much time with you or on the dramatics. I need to know when was the last time you saw Danee and have you talked to Keith?" I questioned. Ceeda started speaking up a lot quicker than DeWhite.

"Yesterday, when Keith brought the girls over to play with Danee, was the last time I saw her. I had a headache and drifted off to sleep while they were here. When DeWhite got home, he woke me up and Danee was gone. I've been calling Keith ever since, and his phone has been off. I went to his mom's along with a couple of his other relatives' house this morning, but nobody has heard or saw him."

"Wait what, you mean his relatives? I thought yawl were siblings. Y'all don't have the same relatives?" DeWhite questioned. Rich let out a slight chuckle. I know he was thinking the same thing I was. This foo had to be dumber than a box of rocks if he thought Ceeda and Keith were blood brother and sister. Some people are so gotdamn stupid it should be a crime.

"We are not real siblings, but I mean we are close like it." Ceeda timidly said.

"Close like that? What the fuck is that supposed to mean? You introduced him as your fucking brother so that's who I thought he was. You had this random dude around my kids and yawl not even related. What type of shit are you on, Ceeda? You don't even know what type of person he really is, yet you lead me on to believe he was your blood." DeWhite was cussin Ceeda out but I blamed him just as much as I blamed her because he was supposed to have done his research before having anyone around them kids.

"My man, you can't sit here and put all the blame on her. You ain't have no business leaving my kids with this bitch no way when she doesn't even take care of her own son. Bottom line, you were out of line leaving them unattended with her, and now I'mma hold y'all both responsible." I told DeWhite, and yeah, I said my kids because that's what they were to me. The love I have for them was strong as if they came from my sack. The look on his face told me he didn't like when I referred to them as my kids, but he knew better than to argue with that statement.

"You never even told me you had any kids when I asked you. Bitch,

I should…" DeWhite charged towards Ceeda, and Rich grabbed him up.

"Now ain't the time to try to fuck her up. Bring your ass on so we can go find My daughter. Oh, and bitch, bring your ass, too." I said as I looked towards Ceeda and nodded my head towards the front door. She immediately hopped up and headed outside. I had Ceeda sit up front with Rich, and I sat in the back with DeWhite. Just in case either of them wanted to try anything, we both would have the ability to prevent it.

After making a few calls, we were informed to go check Ceeda's baby's dad Pete's house because that's where he was at earlier today. Pulling up, Ceeda just dropped her head because she knew damn well where we were. I don't know if it was guilt or embarrassment, but either way, I know she was feeling real low right about now.

Rich stepped out of the car first, and I instructed Ceeda's ass to follow him. I pulled out my gun and told DeWhite to get his bitch ass out, too. Wasn't no need for him to start acting all scared now. He wasn't scared when he left my baby at his crib with this rat ass bitch. Rich hit the door twice and the nigga Pete opened without even checking to see who it was. That's a big ass no, no where I'm from.

We all rushed in, and I closed the door behind me. Pete looked back and forth between all of us. He was confused and scared all at the same time. Not knowing if Ceeda had us come over here or what.

"What. What's up. Ceeda why, you bring these people over here?" Pete questioned Ceeda.

"I didn't, Pete," Ceeda said about to cry.

"Shut up, bitch. You don't need to speak unless I tell you to. Your dumb ass has done enough for the day." Ceeda just didn't know how close she was to meeting her maker with her dumb ass.

"I'm here to see about Keith. Where he's at? Is he upstairs? He got something that belongs to me. Something very valuable and I want it now." I informed Pete.

"Look, I don't know what the hell Keith don got himself into, but I don't even get down like that no more. Me and Keith only speak or see each other every so often. Ever since he got on that powder, I try to steer clear of him cause he's not the same. He dropped by here earlier high off that shit and asked could I look after his girls for a few hours. I told him I couldn't at first, cause I knew he was high and probably wouldn't be back anytime soon, but when he told me his mom was in the hospital and there was no one to look after them, I felt bad. I know when he gets high like that the nigga go too hard, and I didn't want them girls in nobody's trap or running the streets with him. They have been through more than enough in their short lives." Pete explained.

"So, you don't know where he is, and where's the kids?" Rich spoke up.

"No, I don't. His daughters are upstairs sleeping in my son's room. Yawl are more than welcome to go look around and verify that he's nowhere in here. I don't want anything to do with no funny business when it comes to where I lay my head. I got a son to raise, and I been walked away from the bullshit. The only reason I opened the door this late cause I thought it was my chick; she supposed to be on her way over here." Pete was really pleading his case.

Rich gave me a look and headed up the steps to look around. When he yelled down that it was only three kids, I automatically knew that meant Danee wasn't there. Meaning she still had to be with Keith.

"Well, we're going to get out of here, and if I find out you lying about not knowing anything I will be back. That's not a threat, that's a promise." I gave him eye contact and said.

"I swear to God you got my word on this. I just wanna raise my son, that's it, man. That's it." He said with his hands raised as if he was surrendering. I gave him a head nod and we all walked out leaving the door open behind us.

Something was telling me to go to Keith's momma's house. If the mom was in the hospital, he stupid enough to go back to her house especially if he's high. People don't think straight when they get too far gone and I'm sure he's past that point. I told Rich to go by Keith's mom's house before we started a mad manhunt around the city wasting valuable time.

When we pulled on the block, Ceeda gasped for air like she had just seen a ghost. My guess was because there was a car in the driveway.

"What was that for?" Rich questioned.

"That's his car right there; he's gotta be here." Ceeda said excitedly.

Rich parked the car a couple of houses down, and we all got out the car. Ceeda took the lead for some reason, but I was ok with it. If she knocked, he would probably open the door a lot faster anyway. I'm still sticking with the story that she knows what's going on and can't nobody tell me anything different. DeWhite was walking pretty quick, too, but I'm sure he was truly concerned about Danee. No matter how careless he was with her, that's still his biological daughter.

Ceeda knocked on the door and Keith opened up like he was John Gotti, looking all zooted out like he was awaiting our arrival with a pistol in hand.

"Bout muthafuckin time! Took yawl long enough!" Keith said with his chest poked out.

DEWHITE

If he wouldn't have had a gun in his hand, I would've punched that bitch nigga right in his face. I wanted to crack his damn jaw for taking my daughter and running off with her like she was some sort of random or something. Keith had me fooled; I really thought he was an honest, good dude who only wanted to raise his kids and stay out the way, but boy was I wrong. Ceeda's hoe ass had me confused as well. All this time, she was portraying to be someone she wasn't. I'm starting to believe I was sleeping with the enemy.

When Kilo and Rich showed up to my door, I thought it was just going to be for the protection of Monee, but had I known they were going to take us on this ride as well, I would've called the police when Monee showed up to my place. The way Kilo had been talking and swinging his gun around all night, I didn't know if he was going to shoot or what. As bad as I feel about the whole situation, I'm not trying to lose my life over a mistake Ceeda made.

Ceeda walked into the house first, then Rich, me, and finally Kilo. The way Keith greeted us, it was as if he already knew Rich and Kilo, so there were a number of things going through my head. I just needed to get to the bottom line of where my daughter was.

"So, where do we start? Big Boss Rich, finally we meet face to face.

Never thought you'd have to face me after the bullshit you did, now did you? I know you couldn't have possibly thought I would really let you get away with doing my fiancé the way you did. You did her dirty. Yeah, real dirty, and now it's finally time that you pay for what you did."

Keith yelled with spit flying from his mouth. He looked like a fucking lunatic if you ask me. I didn't know if he was talking out the side of his head because he was high or had Rich really done something to his fiancé. Last I knew, she was dead, so he had to be hallucinating or something.

"Bitch nigga shut the fuck up. Ain't nobody do shit to your hoe ass fiancé. Your coward ass really mapped out a whole crime that I never even committed. You're so desperate to ruin my life cause yours is fucked up you tried to pin that shit on me, but it ain't work. How, you feel now bitch? I was never worried about seeing you face to face; cause I know in reality you don't want no smoke. It's that Tony Montana that got you feeling like you on top of the world. How many lines did you blow to give you this much courage, huh?" Rich responded while stepping into Keith's face. Rich had to be just as much of a lunatic as Keith because Keith was holding a gun. I'm sure Rich had one as well, but it wasn't drawn.

Things were starting to make a little more sense, but I was still confused. I pieced together that Keith was blaming Rich for the death of his fiancé, and Rich was denying it. I would be mad, too, if I felt someone killed my fiancé, but I still didn't understand what that had to do with me. Why would Keith drag me and my daughter in the middle of their war when Rich has two daughters of his own? He could've taken one of his kids instead of mine.

Keith looked as if he had said all he had to say and was waiting for someone else to speak. Those drugs must have really been doing a number on him; the man couldn't even think straight enough to carry on a conversation. I noticed Ceeda took a seat and steered clear of the direction of the gun. She was for sure trying to make sure she was safe. I blame all of this on her; if she would've never introduced me to Keith as her brother, we would never be here. I tried to walk toward the couch Ceeda was seated on, and I felt Kilo pull my shirt back in his direction. I didn't know it, but he was using me to hide the gun he had. He must've wanted Keith to feel like he was in charge and surprise him. I just hoped when shots do start ringing out in this bitch, I'm not hit being his shield.

"Now that you got what you want, and that was to see my brah face to face, give us what we want. Where is Danee?" Kilo finally spoke up.

"I'll never have what I want; he took that from me, so I'm taking everything y'all love one by one from y'all." Keith was real bold, threatening them. It was two against one, and regardless if he had a gun or not, he's high. Keith had to know that, if they wanted to, they could've jumped his ass at any moment. I'm sure someone would've got shot for sure, but he would still get his ass whooped.

"Stop with all that big talk. I don't give a fuck about none of that shit. Where is my muthafuckin daughter?" Kilo barked.

"Your daughter? Last I checked, she belonged to Monee and DeWhite. Since you are playing stepdad, you wanna take claims? You weren't taking claims when you was fucking Ceeda now were you? Oh, yawl thought I didn't know? Yeah, DeWhite, did Ceeda tell you how she used to fuck around with Kilo? That's the real reason she started fucking around with your square ass to get back at Monee. You were originally just a pawn in her game to get back at Monee for taking Kilo from her. Another thing is it backfired cause Monee didn't give a fuck."

Keith let out a devilish laugh, but he was the only one in the room who found anything funny. I turned toward Ceeda and gave her a death stare. I should've known she was up to something. She was too desperate to be with me, and I never showed her the same interest, but that only made her try even harder. After so long, I gave in and just started going with the flow, only to find out now that it was all a part of her plan.

"WHERE THE FUCK IS DANEE?" Kilo yelled. It was obvious his patience was running thin with Keith. I could feel the heat radiating off of his body behind me. My nerves started getting the best of me because there was no sign of my daughter being here, and she wasn't with Pete. I automatically began to think the worst. Maybe he already killed her or did something to her where we will never find her as revenge for his fiancé's death.

POP! POP!

"FUCK!" I yelled as I felt a burning sensation in my left shoulder. Keith had let off two shots and one hit me. He was aiming for Kilo, but I was standing right in front of him. When Kilo noticed Keith had grown some balls, he threw me to the side and fired back.

POW! POW! POW!

"AHHHH!" Keith screamed. His body flew back and the gun he was holding flew out his hand. Rich kicked it away from his reach and walked past him. Every shot that Kilo let off hit Keith in a different part of his body. I wanted to know if Kilo's aim was so good, why didn't he just kill him.

"You just don't know when to shut the fuck up and cooperate. I asked you the same question more than once, and I'm not one for repeating myself when it comes to me talking to another grown ass man. Now, your problem you have with Rich ain't have nothing to do with my daughter. She's an innocent child. Just like your, two little girls are. How would you feel if I told you I already made a pit stop over Pete's to handle that before I came to see you? Maybe they'll have the chance to be with their mommy again since daddy ain't doing shit right here on earth."

The look on Keith's face turned from Billy bad ass to a scared ass coward. I knew Kilo was only fucking with his head, because I was with him at Pete's, and he wasn't even the one who saw his kids. Rich did, and they left them asleep. Keith didn't know that, and he let Kilo's words sink in. I noticed tears falling from his face.

No matter how hard he was trying to hold everything inside and look tough, he couldn't any longer. Rich walked back into the living room and shook his head. He walked in the other direction of the house with a gun now in hand that he wasn't showing before. Ceeda still was sitting in place on the couch not saying a word. I couldn't believe she was sitting back like she was all innocent, and she should've been the person to take the first bullet, not me.

Rich walked back into the room and, before he could say another word, I heard another gunshot. Ceeda screamed and began to cry.

Looking over, I saw Keith's brains scattered against the wall and his lifeless body sitting there. Rich then turned the gun towards Ceeda. She started pleading for her life and apologizing saying how everything was a misunderstanding. She even promised to skip town and never be seen around here again. Rich never said a word. I closed my eyes and heard another shot. I was too nervous to open them to see what he had done to Ceeda because I no longer heard her cries.

"I found Danee. She's in there sleeping so there wasn't a need to keep him alive. We got what we came here for." Rich said, and I opened my eyes. A smile crept across my face, and I was no longer focused on the pain I felt in my shoulder. Rich turned back towards the direction he had just come from. Kilo turned towards me and a slight smirk was on his face. I knew he was happy to have found Danee just like me. It was now time for us to get out of here. I needed to get to a hospital, and Danee needed to get home to her worried momma.

"I know you don't think everything is sweet."

"What, you mean? We got Danee; there's no beef here. We have a common ground and that's my kids. Whatever problems we had before tonight, let just let bygones be bygones." I didn't really know Kilo to have a serious beef with him outside of him being with the mother of my kids, but I was willing to drop that now that he helped find my daughter.

"Bygones, huh? Nigga, there was never no beef between us. I don't have beef. If there's a problem, I solve it, and you, my friend, have become a problem." Kilo said and everything went in slow motion after that. I heard two shots. I saw sparks from the gun and everything went black.

KILO

After grabbing Danee out of Rich's arms, I felt like there was a weight lifted off my shoulders. I would've never been able to forgive myself had something happened to her, and I promised her mom I would handle it. Up until tonight, I had never claimed Monee's kids as my own, but they were indeed just as much mine as hers. Birthday parties, doctor's appointments, school activities, sick night, and school projects, I'm there through it all. I'll be damned if I sat back and let the police find my daughter when I'm able.

Danee was sleeping, and she appeared to be unbothered, but I wouldn't know until we got her home and she woke up. Thank goodness she sleeps as hard as she does. I didn't want to wake her in the house, and she witnessed the amount of blood. That would be too traumatizing for a little girl her age. I didn't want to mentally fuck her up for good; she had already experienced a scare being with this man for the past twenty-four or so hours. I can only imagine what types of shit he did in front of her or said. Danee isn't exposed to a lot of things, and we wanted to keep it that way. She deserves to keep her innocence as long as possible.

When I went to place Danee in the backseat of Rich's car, she was startled from her sleep. She practically jumped out of my arms until she realized who I was.

"It's ok, baby. I'm taking you home to your mom."

"Dad. Can I call you daddy, Mr. Kilo?" Danee innocently asked.

"Of course, you can." I proudly replied. Danee just didn't know how much that meant to me that she wanted to acknowledge me as her dad.

"I wanna go home. I don't ever wanna come over Mr. Keith's again. And I don't wanna go over my real dads either. I just wanna stay with you, mommy, and DJ." Danee said while reaching to give me a hug around my neck.

"Don't worry, baby. You never have to see either of them ever again if you don't want to." I said to her as if she had an option.

"I love you, daddy."

"I love you, too, baby." I gave her a kiss on her forehead and fastened her seatbelt before closing the door and getting in the front seat.

On the way to the crib, I thought about everything that took place today. Monee didn't want me to leave the house at first, but had I not gone against her word and left out, I would've never seen Keith out with Danee and found out what was going on. Sometimes, we just have to go against the grain and follow our first mind. I know Monee was pissed at me at first, but it ended up being what was best for our family in the end.

Pulling up to the house, I noticed there were still a few lights on. Rich left his car running and went inside to help Monica grab the girls, so they could head home. I appreciated Rich and Monica for being there for us. Monica was there holding her sister down, and Rich was by my side holding me down. That's what family is about and for. Being there when you really need each other.

I grabbed Danee and headed inside the house. I told her to go shower and I would leave her night clothes out on her bed for when she was done. I planned to talk to her about everything that happened once she was done but while she was doing that I headed into D-Man's room to see if he was still awake.

Like always, D-Man was in the toy room on the game playing with his eyes glued to the TV.

"Aye! My man, I need you to turn that off and get in the shower. It's time for bed." I told him and, without any backtalk, he did as he was told.

"Is my sister home? Did yawl find her?" He asked.

"Yeah, your sister's in the bathroom showering."

"Is she ok?" He asked with concern laced in his voice.

"Yeah, she's good. She's better now that she's home. Go to the other bathroom and take care of your business. I'mma grab your night clothes and when you're done getting dressed, go in our room and get in our bed."

D-Man gave me a head nod and walked away. One thing I can say, these two kids are two of the most respectful kids I've ever come across considering the level of filter Monee's mouth has. You would expect them to be some real-life assholes but they're not.

I had a seat downstairs in the living room and waited for Danee to finish getting dressed for bed. When she came downstairs, I could see in her eyes she was tired, so I planned to keep it quick.

"Baby, let me ask you a few things, then I promise you can go get in our bed with mommy."

"Ok." She said it sounding so sweet.

"Did Keith touch any of your no-no areas?"

"No."

"Did he hit you or yell at you?"

"He didn't hit me, but he yelled at me when I told him I wanted to go home."

"Did Keith say anything to you or do anything that you think was bad?" I didn't want to bluntly ask her was the nigga snorting power or making transactions in front of her, so I had to sugar coat it to the best of my ability.

"No, but he didn't feed me anything but ships and juice. I told him those were snacks, but he yelled at me again."

"Ok, are you hungry now? Do you want me to make you something to eat really quick?"

"No, I just wanna go to sleep. But can we have pancakes for breakfast with bacon?" She smiled when she put in her request for breakfast.

"We sure can; that's not a problem. Is there anything you think D-Man or Mommy might want for breakfast?"

"Ummm, I think Jr will want eggs, cause he always likes eggs with his pancakes and Mommy is going to want some strawberries with her." She knew her mom and brother well cause that's exactly what they ate.

"Sounds like a deal. I'll handle breakfast; you just gotta worry about eating all your food. Go ahead and get in bed. I love you, and I'll talk to you in the morning." I gave her a kiss on the forehead and a hug.

"Love you, too, daddy. Good night!" She said and ran upstairs to my bedroom.

While everyone in the house was sleeping peacefully, I couldn't. The sight of Keith and DeWhite's lifeless body was stuck in my head. Not that killing them was taunting me or anything, I just couldn't believe I had to resort to my old ways. I took a double shot of D'usse and headed upstairs to take my shower and rinse off today's sins.

As the steaming hot water ran down my body, I said a silent prayer to the Lord to forgive me for my sins and understand that I was doing as a man was supposed to do to protect his family. I also asked that he wrap his arms around my family and keep us together. I asked for strength, love, loyalty, and growth within my household and said my Amen. When I stepped out of the shower, I dried off and threw on my draws, some basketball shorts, and a wife beater. I thought I heard Monee moving in the room, but I wasn't sure, so I continued on what I was doing. I reached down to grab my dirty clothes from the floor and couldn't believe my eyes.

Waking up with Jr on one side of me and Danee on the other, it felt as if I was in a dream. I rubbed both of their backs and kissed them multiple times. It still seemed unreal. I don't even remember falling asleep; I was crying so hard in fear for my baby girl's life I must have passed out. Both Danee and Jr were bathed and neatly dressed in their night clothes smelling good. Kilo must've placed them in the bed with me because the last thing I remember was me laying on the bed talking to Monica crying. Knowing that Kilo did whatever he had to do to get my daughter back home safe to us made me love him a thousand times more. I don't know what, how, or when he did it, but he made sure it was done.

Lord knows I would've broken down had I woke up tomorrow morning and she was still missing. It was hard enough being a mother and feeling helpless to my child. The pain I felt tonight not knowing if my daughter was safe or being mistreated, I wouldn't wish on my worst enemy. I couldn't believe that her own father would put her in that type of situation, to begin with. I'm not going to dwell on it because it's done and over with. I said a silent prayer to God thanking him for his protection and being here for my family and I, before slowly getting up off the bed. I tried to be as gentle as I could, so I wouldn't wake the kids.

"Kilo?" I called out loud enough for him to hear me but not too loud to the point I would wake up the kids.

The bathroom door opened, and he walked out in my direction. I rushed towards him and just started crying tears of joy. If he didn't know how much I appreciated him before, I wanted him to know now. When I wrapped my arms around his ribs and hugged him as tight as I possibly could, I wanted him to feel every emotion I had inside of me. Kilo wrapped his arms back around me and squeezed tight. He placed light kisses on my neck and nestled his head on my shoulder.

"I love you, Nee. I love y'all! With every breath in me. Just know that whatever I gots to do, no matter what it is, I'm going to do it to keep my family together and safe." Kilo said in my ear, only causing me to cry harder. He has told me he loved me probably a thousand times, but I felt it in my soul this time when he spoke to me. I got chills all over my body hearing him say those words.

"I love you, too, baby. I love you so much, and I appreciate any and everything you do and have done for us." I replied between tears. I felt him let go of me and push me back a little catching me off guard some.

"Babe, is there something you want to tell me?" Kilo asked in a serious tone, and I was totally lost as to what he was asking me this question for, especially right now.

"No!" I replied with my face scrunched up some still trying to hold onto him. But he had let go completely.

When I noticed he had a pregnancy test in his hand, I dropped my head. I had totally forgotten that was even in the bathroom and the situations that took place earlier tonight because of everything going on. I took a deep breath and let out a sigh. Kilo looked at me with a confused look on his face, and I didn't know whether he was disappointed or really confused.

"Talk to me, Nee; what's going on?" Kilo asked.

"I don't know what to say, Kilo."

"What you mean you don't know what to say. Is this your test or Monica's?"

"It's mine. I know now is not the right time, so I understand if you don't want to keep it. With everything going on, I totally forgot I even took the test earlier after you left. I originally planned to tell you once you got home, but you woke me up telling me that Danee was missing and it slipped my mind. I'm sorry, babe." Tears started falling once again.

"Why are you apologizing for? Why ain't now the time? What better time than now to start our family? I'm a grown man. I know what I'm doing each and every time I touch your body. I would never ask you to get rid of a baby we created. It may not be planned, but it's for damn sure not a mistake. If I didn't want any kids and a future with you, we wouldn't be this far." Kilo was speaking to me tonight in ways I never knew he would, and it felt so good to finally have him confirm all the ways he felt about not only me but our family.

He turned and walked away toward the walk-in closet and came back to where I was standing. Grabbing both my hands and looking me in my eyes, I felt like the love I always dreamed of was right here with me. All the love I had inside for him, I wished I could verbally express to him at this moment, but I couldn't.

"Monee, I'm not perfect, nor do I ever want you to believe I am. Shit, I'm not even close to it, but I'm going to try every day to prove my love to you. There's no other woman I'd rather carry my seed and raise a family with. When we first started rocking, I knew there was something different about you; that's the reason that, no matter how many times you tried to cut me off, I wouldn't let you go. We've been building our little empire together now for almost two years, and we got forever to go.

Even if you weren't pregnant right now, I would still feel the same way, but just knowing there's a part of me growing inside of you, I can't wait any longer. I love you for who you are, what you do, and who you've helped me to become. I'm not into all that corny bending down on one knee shit, but you get my drift. I wanna spend the rest of my life with you and you really don't have any other choice, but I'm going to ask you are you ready to change your last name?"

I was speechless because, if you would've told me Kilo would be proposing to me after all the shit, we had experienced in the last twelve hours, I would've laughed in your face.

"Oh my, God, yes, baby. I'm ready to be your wife!" I cried.

While pulling my hands from his and placing them over my mouth, he reached back for my left hand and placed a big ass rock on my ring finger. I don't know much about marriage and I didn't give a fuck what finger he put it on as long as I had it. For all I know, it was supposed to go on my right hand until marriage, but Kilo and I said our vows the moment he told me it was until death.

"I'll rip my heart out and give it to you girl if you needed it. Nee, you just don't know how happy of a man you make me."

"If you needed me to, I would do the same. When I met you, I knew everything about you was real, but I never knew that we would get this deep. I give you my heart and soul. Just promise you'll continue to be the realest on my team."

EPILOGUE: FIVE YEARS LATER

Time flies when you're having fun is what they always say, and I can't disagree. Kilo and I've been real busy over the past five years. Two kids, a ring, and another kid on the way is a whole lot since the night he saved Danee. It's safe to say he wants to keep me barefoot and pregnant. Kilo Jr and Kania are damn near twins, the only thing is they are exactly a year apart and the opposite sex. How the hell I managed to have two kids with the same exact birthday beats me. I guess that's what I get for not listening to the doctor when he told me to wait my six weeks.

That man has some strong ass genes, I'm hoping this little girl comes out looking something like me. I'm the one carrying these babies and doing all the work but it's not showing one bit. Danee and DJ are growing so fast and extremely helpful when it comes to the younger two kids. Kilo Jr and Kania for sure have their fathers' attitude and temper. Sometimes I don't know if I'm raising kids or two damn adults around here.

As I expected Kilo is a wonderful father and husband. You would think that we have five kids together and that my oldest two were biologically his as well with the bond they share. It's amazing seeing my kids happy even though their father is dead. Danee and DJ both call Kilo dad and consider him to be their father. Since I was pregnant with Kilo Jr it's been that way. I mean he is the only man who has been here for them so 'I'm ok with it.

DeWhite's death was no surprise to me nor did I feel one ounce of sympathy for him. You would think I would've been more affected by it, but I wasn't. Our history meant nothing when my child's safety got involved. My kids were a little hurt at first but they got over it rather quickly. I believe the fact that Kilo was actually there for them more than DeWhite had ever been made their transition easier.

After having Kania, Kilo and I got married. I was engaged for what seemed like forever, but I refused to walk down the aisle pregnant. The wedding was small but everything I dreamed of. Just close family and friends. We didn't even have a honeymoon, but I did get the new Tahoe I asked for a while back. As of right now, we are waiting for the new house to be completed so we can move before the baby is born. There was no way we can stay in the house we originally purchased together because we outgrew that house two kids ago. I would've never in my wildest dreams imagined having three more kids so our first house was purchased with only four tenants in mind. I guess God and Kilo had other plans for my life and body.

Business, of course, expanded. That one daycare is now a chain of six and the elderly group home we have is doing wonderfully. The fellas are still sticking to their same businesses. Kilo said he'd rather invest in the stock market than to open another business so that's his new venture, let's hope everything goes well with this.

Monica and Rich are still Monica and Rich. They still have the two girls and Rich is trying to convince Monica to give him another child but she's not in agreeance. I don't blame her because after her last pregnancy she went through a bad case of Postpartum depression. Rich doesn't understand that so I'm sure he will continue to pressure her but who knows.

All in all, I'm finally happy. No drama, no stress just living my life and taking care of my family. Something I've always wanted to do but never seems to be able to. I couldn't ask for a better friend, lover, provider, father and most importantly husband than Kilo. It took a lot of shit for us to get to the point we are today. You never know how far love will go if you never give it a change. Like Kilo always tells me sometimes your wife is the realest on your team, and I owe him credit for that. Real recognized real and after falling in love with the realest there was no going back!

The End

CLOSING REMARKS FROM CHANIQUE J

They say, when it's real, you know, but sometimes the timing just isn't right. That doesn't mean that person isn't for you. It just means when y'all tried the timing was off. Don't get me wrong, I'm not saying wait for that one person you feel is Mr. or Mrs. "Right" forever because they just may not be it. What I am saying is no one is perfect, but you have to be able to love through those imperfections. Stop looking for relationship idols and goals from social media or basing your relationship on other couples and create your own. No two relationships are the same, no matter how many similarities they share. Why not break the mold and do the unthinkable?

When a person is real, and what they feel is genuine, you can feel that shit. They don't have to tell you all the time, granted, it feels good to hear. Actions always speak louder than words any day. If you're going to give your energy to a relationship, don't half-step or give a part of you, give your all. Whether that person gives the same in return or not, this isn't your problem in the end if there is an end. Because, the ultimate reward to self will be that you always gave your best, so you'll have no regrets. My advice to you is, love without a limit and enjoy life while you're doing it.

Again, thanks for rocking with me, and I hope you all enjoyed this read.

If you haven't already be sure to check out my other work

NO LOVE GIVEN 1-4 (COMPLETE SERIES)

Crazy About Your Love 1&2 (Complete Series)

No We Without You and I 1&2 (Complete Series)
Fistful of Love Volume 2 (Anthology)
Loving Everything About My Savage 1&2 (Complete Series)

www.ingramcontent.com/pod-product-compliance
Lightning Source LLC
Chambersburg PA
CBHW052009150726
47999CB00004B/1589